To Christine, Joe, and Nick—
To the moon and back . . .

To Mrs. C,   5-11-13

THE
NITWITS
COME
TO TOWN,

Time for
a Monkey Scrub!
Watchout!

JIM CHRISMAN

Enjoy!

CONTENTS

1	They Call Themselves Nitwits	1
2	Go Rake the Leaves	11
3	Doing the Robot	19
4	Get! Get! Get!	33
5	The 'S' Word	41
6	Flippin' Burgers	47
7	Playin' Ball	55
8	Postal Service	65
9	Try It; You Might Like It	73
10	Something's Fishy	83
11	Growth Spurt	95
12	Say Cheese	107
13	Wasn't Even His Birthday	111
14	The 'Last' Pop-Tart	123
15	No Cat's Meow	133
16	Pucker Up	143
	Acknowledgments	153

1

THEY CALL THEMSELVES NITWITS

In this story there is a dead cat, a sloppy kiss, a sloppy side yard full of doll heads, and a whole bunch of other stuff. The dead cat is my friend's and the sloppy kiss, well it's not mine thank God, but I'm planning it. It involves my sisters. It is so awesome. It hasn't happened yet. I want it to happen tonight. I'm arranging it. It is going to be so epic. I have to get back at my sisters; I have to!

Oh, and I'll tell you about the doll heads and all the other stuff. I'll make you see why the kiss is so great, not that I like kisses, and I'm sure my sisters won't like this one either!

I'm getting a little ahead of myself. I have to tell you why tonight is happening tonight. Oh, it's going to be great. It has to work. It will work.

Okay, I have to tell you what is going on, and to do so I have to give you a little background first. Here I go:

First off, I thought *my* family was crazy. I'm Joe, Joe Christmas, I live at, well, I'm not going to tell you; I'm going to make up a street. There are suspicious strangers out there and I'm sure some will eventually be reading this and I don't want them to know where I live. There is a lesson for you young readers, and I hope your mom will appreciate the fact you've learned something in this book because I'm telling you it sure gets crazy in these pages and your moms might not like that. I'm going to tell you about my neighbors, the Nitwits. They're the ones that made me change my mind about my family. Sure my family is odd and weird and just like yours I'm sure, and annoying, yes, my sisters . . . uhh-hhh! My sisters!!! A-NOY-ING. (That is not misspelled; when sounding it out, you don't need both n's!) But the Nitwits—they're crazy, and I'll get back to them in a second.

About me, I live in one of those old houses with the porch that goes all around it (well used to, I'll get back to that, too), and it has a basement and an attic and a whole lot of other stuff, but that's not important now. What is important is that you know that there is a whole bunch of people that live in my house. See, I live with three older sisters, and one male cousin, Brent (who goes in and out at all hours), and one aunt (who is not Brent's mom), and my parents of course. We have two dogs, a turtle somewhere, and a hamster. The hamster is Aggie's, the sister closest in age to me. I think Cuddles is the fifth or sixth hamster she's had, all named Cuddles of course.

Oh duh, and my grandparents. They aren't married—they're not divorced either. See, each is from my parents. One is from my mom and one is from my dad, or I guess you can reverse that and say my parents are from them. Whatever, one is my dad's dad and the other is my mom's mom.

So you see, there are a lot of people at my house and where there are a lot of people . . . well . . . things can get pretty crazy, but that doesn't mean we are crazy.

Here's a crazy story, or what I used to think was a crazy story. Okay, it still may be a crazy story, but it does not mean we are crazy like the Nitwits. This is it, to show you what I mean. One time Gramps, my dad's dad, came home with sixteen trout he and his old buddies had caught. Of course Gramps didn't wrap them up nicely or anything and, when he came home, he covered everything in the house with trout-splash, and he dropped one or two fish, and the dogs ran around the house sharing one, and Grandma slipped and fractured her elbow (I think it was her ulna), and my sister Cece (my middle sister) knocked over a scented candle trying to corner Inca, our older dog, and a drape caught on fire. Gramps doused it with . . . guess what Gramp's doused it with. Go ahead and guess. See if you can get it right. Well, here it is: He doused it with fishy ice water he had in his cooler that was keeping the trout fresh. I bet most of you guessed it right; however, there was no ice in the chest and the freshness . . . well. Crazy, you think? Normal crazy is what I say. Let me break it down:

Gramps brought home his trout; it was a sloppy mess. The dogs took advantage. Grandma was caught by the dogs being dogs. Cece tried to help. She knocked over one of Aunt Jesse's candles. Gramps thought quickly, even though everything stunk like fish guts for awhile. That is it—crazy yeah, but definitely normal crazy.

So yeah, our house can get crazy, but I think, talking to my friends, Eddie and Beep, that our house is normal crazy. (By the way, Beep's real name is Collin, but he says "beep" all the time so we call him Beep. He says beep because he says things like 'What the beep' and 'No beep' whenever he is animated. His mom doesn't want him to have a potty-mouth but he sure seems to have a potty-brain, so all the beeps.) Things like trout-splash happen at their houses too, but nothing, I mean nothing is normal crazy at my neighbor's, the Nitwits. They have been here close to a year and it is only crazy and crazier all the time. They have a big house like ours and a big family like ours . . . well, not *like* ours at all, but a big house and lots of people going in and out. Yeah, it is only since the Nitwits moved in that St. Brigid's Hospital stations an ambulance down the street most every day.

The Nitwits are crazy.

There is no way I can tell you all of it here. I'm not sure if I can even remember it all or get it all in order, but I do have plenty of pictures; it's a hobby of mine, but I don't put the date stamp on it or anything and they are all kind of in a box, but they're great! I'll show them to you if I get a chance. I have to find the box. I have one of those cameras that takes film, and I have a little dark room I made in the basement. Mom likes that I do things "old school." The box of the Nitwit pics has to be somewhere. I should—

Oh No!

"Gramps! Gramps please don't do that! Gramps!"

Too late, Gramps has just found a leftover burrito in the fridge. I don't know why I am writing in the kitchen, but at least I will get an early start. Let me break it down:

The burrito was probably Brent's, my cousin. He comes in late all the time, like two-three in the morning. He is so tired so he forgets everything. Gramps is so excited or should I say eeee-vil. (Say eeee-vil like an old-time vampire. That is the type of evil I'm talking about.) He is going to eat the burrito. (It's probably from Sombrero's; those are sooooo good.) Gramps is going to eat the burrito and, when he does, I have to go put up the tents in the backyard. Yeah, I bet you can guess this one . . . and multiply it by one hundred.

Gramps has a room on the first floor; we have three floors, not counting the attic, the basement, and Dad's secret cellar that he shows to everyone that comes over, so it's hardly secret. He tells people his middle name is *Montresor* (it's from

5

an Edgar Allan Poe story) when he shows them it. He gets a big laugh out of it; he alone. He does the whole *muhahaha* thing. I just shake my head.

Well, Gramps is on the first floor and let me tell you, we'll be in the tents for two days. I swear, my friend Beep said it was like the time he found a dead cat in a culvert near Monkey Stream. Its real name, even though it is a river, is Monche (Mahn-chee) Stream, but we call it Monkey; it sounds better, especially when you say I jumped in the Monkey or I'm Monkey soaked or we are eating Monkey fish tonight. I can't shorten it and call it monkfish because that is a real fish, and I said we were eating monkfish one time and Grandma got all excited but it was just trout and she cried in her room for three days. I had to go to the store and ask for monkfish everyday until they got some and I had to buy it with my own money. It was disgusting.

What's great about all the Monkey Stream stuff is that my sisters hate it. However, there is a cool place to swim there and there is fishing and a little south of here is a campground and stuff and they go there all the time with their friends and all the high school boys. The high school boys always say things about monkeys and stuff. It certainly doesn't bother my sisters then . . . sisters . . . uhhhhh.

The whole *monkey* thing really bothers and confuses the Nitwits. They have a problem when words are like that. I think that is the most important thing to know about them. They have a real big—

"Gramps! Seriously don't eat that!"

Gramps gave me a look. I'm not going to say anything else to him. He is old, but he is tough—ex-Marine.

I moved to the dining room. Let's see, the Nitwits, I was saying words really get to them, kind of like the way beans get to Gramps and then I get to the tents. I have all the outdoor chores just because I am a boy. Seriously, my sisters always tell my parents to make me do the outside chores because I'm a boy. They say it all the time, so I have all the outside chores, but I do my own laundry too. I can't stand all the extra flowery stuff my sisters put in the washer and oh, it's bleach city for Grandma and Gramps and Aunt Jess.

"Gramps!"

I've got to go.

He's following me. Right now I'm in the Florida room or California room or some state room my grandma calls it; it's in the back left of our house and Gramps has brought in a steaming plate of burrito. He chops it up to make it easier to eat. I'd try to take it away from him, but for one he is old and he enjoys it, and two, he is way too strong for me to do anything, still—an ex-Marine.

I think he knows I am writing about him. He just laughed at me and ate his beany burrito bites. He really is still real strong, really. He was in the Navy. Marines are part of the Navy right? Maybe not; no, I don't think so, but I'm sure he was at sea a bunch. I should know; he's my gramps. Maybe he was a Seal. He definitely was in some sort of tough guy Special Ops that is for sure. I just hope he wasn't on a submarine for any length of time . . . for everyone else's sake.

I'm in the tent now. I won't be able to get my sisters back tonight. I will have to do it some other time. Gramps! I can hear Gramps laughing in his room. My sisters are mad at me—it's supposed to rain tonight. I had to put the flysheet over their tent. At least I have my own backpacking tent so I don't have to be in their bag of perfume.

I'm good at the tent stuff on account of Gramps gets into some sort of bean (black, pinto, refried, kidney, garbanzo) about once a month. It stinks, literally and figuratively. See, I like burritos and one of Mom's pizza concoctions has garbanzos on it and Dad likes some Italian bean soup. We all like tacos with beans and rice, and lentils (those work for Gramps too). There is this red lentil chowder sort of thing that Brent came home with from some Indian place, yum! Well, if we don't eat all the beans and lentils when Mom cooks them (or the one time a year my sisters actually cook something besides oatmeal or Cup-O-Noodles) yep, you guessed it, Gramps finds it, and we are in the tents. He's supposed to be on a fixed diet, but Gramps is not going to go without. 'It's a cross I'll bear,' he says and laughs as he snatches a bean-filled leftover.

Oh yeah, when Beep found that dead cat, he brought it over in a wagon. Well, it must have been fresh because a day or two later, yeah, that is what Gramps is about: perfume de dead cat.

Gramps won't take any medicine or anything. Grandma doesn't seem to mind. She won't leave the house when he is in his condition. I think it's because she has so much of her medicines on her that she rubs all over herself everyday with these little pads that she leaves all over her room (I'll get to that later). All those salves and stuff, they make my cheeks tingle, itch, and then turn red when she wants one of her Joe hugs and smashes me all against her. The coughs and tears aren't far behind either. It's brutal. I itch for days.

Grandma kind of smells like those cakes in the public bathroom urinals. Not that I've ever meant to smell them or have investigated the little cakes, but you guys know. I hope it's only you guys.

My sister Trudy, the oldest one, probably knows what I mean, yeah. She had to go into the men's bathroom at the local small plane airport not the giant international one. It was a hazing thing for some club at high school. She had to go in there and ask for directions to the girls' bathroom. Stupid, I know. They wanted to embarrass her—some *friends*. See she had to go in, shout out the question loud enough so her *friends* could hear it, and then get an answer. They saw some guy go in and they sent her in a few seconds later. It took like five minutes. She stood in the men's bathroom for five minutes yelling: "Where is the women's bathroom?" It took her that long because the only guy in the bathroom was deaf. Can you believe it? When he came out of the stall, he went a bit crazy because Trudy was in there, but Trudy actually knows some sign language and she was able to get him to calm down, and he was cool with it and actually signed to her friends that the girls' bathroom was right next door.

She did all that and she didn't even join the club. Smart move.

Back to the Nitwits, they are crazy; I have a billion things in my head about them, but I think I'll start with a story about Lil' Bro Nitwit.

Lil' Bro Nitwit, yeah, that is his name, not my nickname for him. They call him that, the Nitwits. He's Lil' Bro Nitwit and there is Big Bro Nitwit, Big Sis Nitwit, Grandpa Nitwit, Grandma Nitwit, Mom Nitwit, Dad Nitwit, Uncle Nitwit, and Aunt Nitwit. That's what they call themselves. I've never heard it different. It is not even Uncle Stu or Uncle Stu Nitwit even, or Lil' Bro or Lil' Bro Robby or Lil' Bro Robby Nitwit. Nope, it is plain old Nitwit. (By the way, I made up those first names.) All I know them by is by Nitwit. I don't know if it's Stu or Robby or Attila or Aphrodite or John-Paul-George-Ringo. All I know is that they answer their phone and introduce themselves with the whole Nitwit thing. There is a story there, more than one, but like I said, I'll start with Lil' Bro Nitwit.

I'll tell more later. Dad wants lights out—school night.

2

Go Rake The Leaves

First, I won't hide it from you; we spent two nights in the tents and now I won't be able to have 'the kiss' happen tonight or tomorrow night either—too much going on, so I'm going to take the time to tell you about the Nitwits. Man, but I can't wait for the kiss; it's going to be epic. I'll have to think of a better time to have it happen, but right now I'll tell you how Lil' Bro Nitwit broke his arm . . . the first time. I think it was the first time. It was the first time I ever saw him break his arm, but then again, they haven't lived here very long.

So the Nitwits, well, words just don't seem to be their strong suit. Sometimes, in one moment, they get what you say or what they say to each other; they understand; they understand the word, then poof, a little magic, a little dark magic (I'm sure it's dark and it is just a little because it is so simple but bad), and none of them get it and one of them breaks his arm or starts a fire or tries to buy candy with a box of nails or picks up a friend and throws him in the bushes. Yeah, that's how it goes. It's crazy, and I am writing this to let you see how crazy the Nitwits are. They're crazy.

For one, my name is Joe as I have told you, and Big Bro Nitwit once in awhile will try to put me in a cup, or pour some sugar on me, or chase me with a spoon so he can 'stir' me, or dump some cream on me—it's ridiculous. C'mon, I'm Joe, Joseph, not a 'cup of joe.' I'm not hot coffee! I'm not even going to get into my last name. It is the words. They get to them. They really get to the Nitwits.

Well, it was autumn and that is when Lil' Bro Nitwit broke his arm. It was a nice day and I was cleaning Dad's Jeep. See, Grandma had wanted roasted chicken and stuff and she didn't know how to turn on the grill with the propane tank and she's not going to touch briquettes and it couldn't be baked. You would think that she would simply ask one of my sisters to go get her a grilled chicken from the grocery store; of course she wouldn't ask them to cook (and they wouldn't, no way, my sisters . . . uhhhhh) but no, Grandma got an idea in her head and she went with it. She didn't know how to light the grill, but she did know how to turn on the Jeep.

Yes, Grandma started the engine of the Jeep, popped the hood open and stuck a whole chicken on the engine.

She added spices and some olive oil; she put some carrots and squash on the radiator; she put pasta near the chicken, at least it was in a pot, and some garlic bread in foil.

So I was cleaning up Grandma's dinner—it was outside, so my job—and I hear Mom Nitwit yell to Lil' Bro Nitwit to rake the leaves.

I don't mind raking leaves—a huge pile and then a hundred jumps into it and another pile and a hundred more jumps into it and then a hundred piles—I can do it all day. It is great. Then, when it is late, I like to sneak into the pile and wait for one of my sisters to come home from a date and, right when she goes to kiss a boy (they do it all the time; this is how I know the kiss will work), I jump out scaring them both, and then my Dad comes out and gives the boy the evil eye, and taps his watch, and points to my sister and then to the house and the boy speeds off, yeah!

Of course, I've never done it—scare them. I always fall asleep in the pile of leaves. I really should wait until curfew to hide in the pile, but I'm afraid that one of my sisters will be coming down the road and see me, so I get in it early. I fall asleep every time, and I get these bites and weird rashes all over, and grandma puts one of her salves on me and I stink for days and they don't even work, and cats follow me all over to school and back, but anyway, I don't mind raking leaves.

Heck, I thought I'd help Lil' Bro Nitwit. They have plenty of trees, but to tell you the truth, there weren't that many leaves on the ground. It was late September and we hadn't had a frost yet. Some leaves still held the color of summer. Oh well, maybe Mom Nitwit really liked a clean lawn.

I went back to work getting the spilled baked beans out of the radiator fan. I didn't even know Grandma put them there until a brown sugary puddle started forming, and that's when I saw Lil' Bro Nitwit with his rake kind of staring up at the trees in front of their house. I guess he wanted to make the leaves fall or something. He was staring at them for a good while.

I busied myself; night was coming, the sun setting like a grapefruit (I just read some newspaper article, in a museum, call the sun a grapefruit, so I had to put it in here, seriously, the sun a grapefruit!) when I heard a *kaflop* or a *thud-flud* or something like that. I ran over to the noise and there Lil' Bro Nitwit was lying on the ground in a tiny splatter of leaves with the rake dangling above him fifteen feet high in the tree. I looked up at the rake, down at him, and back up to the rake.

Was he? Did he?

"Are you alright?" I asked.

"Yeah sure, just a broken arm," Lil' Bro Nitwit said.

"Yeah?" I said. "You really broke your arm?" I was concerned. Here was a little kid in front of me who just broke his arm.

"Yeah, I'm pretty sure I heard a crack and it hurts; it hurts really bad." He shrugged.

He shrugged! I couldn't believe it. I didn't know what to say to that. He was standing there, a broken arm, no crying, no jumping around, no nothing. He just stood there in front of me. I had to say something.

"Well, what happened? What were you doing?" I finally asked.

"Mom Nitwit told me to rake the leaves." He looked at me stupidly, not saying he was stupid looking, but indicating that I was stupid.

"Yeah?"

"Well," he looked up at the tree. He shook his head at me. "That's where they are."

I looked up and back at him. "Yeah," I said.

He pointed up with a finger from his good arm. "That's where the leaves are." He said it like 'duh' was supposed to follow.

I looked back up and then back down to him. That's when Mom Nitwit came out. She made a little commotion. I guess it was nice; she cared . . . a little—you'll see.

"What happened Lil' Bro Nitwit?" she asked.

"I was raking the leaves and fell out of the tree," he said plainly.

I shook my head in disbelief. He had been up the tree raking leaves . . . up the tree!

"Well, Lil' Bro Nitwit," Mom Nitwit said, "you don't rake the leaves in the trees." She was getting into the angry phase that parents get into after they know you won't die and after

15

you've done something stupid . . . but he had a broken arm. Maybe she could wait a little more.

Well, I was thinking yeah, duh, of course you don't rake the leaves in the trees. You rake giant piles to jump in, and when your sisters are really annoying you, you sneak in a little prize from Inca or Casey, my two dogs, and get your sisters to jump into the pile, but they never do, and I always seem to forget what I have put in the pile until I jump in again. I'll tell you this: Never jump into a pile of leaves head first while yelling whoooo-hoooooooo—never!

Now Mom Nitwit kept talking to Lil' Bro Nitwit and this is what is crazy about them. She asked Lil' Bro Nitwit, "What is the windy thing that knocks down so many leaves when it is windy?"

"Um . . . the wind," Lil' Bro Nitwit said.

"Yes, the wind," Mom Nitwit said. "And what does the wind do?"

Lil' Bro Nitwit simply stared.

"Like what Uncle Nitwit does every morning with his nose at 5:15," said Mom Nitwit.

"Blows," said Lil' Bro Nitwit.

"Yes, the wind blows . . . so."

Lil' Bro Nitwit simply stared again.

Mom Nitwit looked like she was going to cuff him on the back of the head. She looked befuddled. She peered into Lil' Bro Nitwit's face. "That's why you don't climb up in the tree with a rake."

"Oh," said Lil' Bro Nitwit.

"You climb up with a blower, a leaf blower," said Mom Nitwit.

"Oh, yeah," Lil' Bro Nitwit said.

I tell you, these Nitwits, crazy right?!

I took a picture of the rake. The Nitwits had left for the doctors when I went to grab my camera. I've got to find that picture. I'm okay organized when it comes to my hobby, but I have to hide all the pictures all the time because of my sisters and Brent but mostly my sisters . . . uhhhhh.

You know, I guess I can boil this down about the Nitwits. If you are ever asked, "Why did Lil' Bro Nitwit fall out of the tree?"

His mom told him to rake the leaves.

3

DOING THE ROBOT

It's been a week. We spent another night in the tents. Mom and Dad don't even try to reason with Gramps anymore; I think they like to camp. Tonight won't work for the kiss: All my sisters are out, out as long as they can be. Well, I might as well tell you more about the Nitwits. It will help you understand how great 'the kiss' is going to be. I mean really, when you get to know the Nitwits and what is going to happen—the kiss will be hilarious, totally hilarious, totally humiliating.

So this is a great one. I saw it; well, I saw part of it. I was on the side yard cleaning up all my sister Aggie's dolls that she beheaded. There must have been around sixty of them. They were strewn all over the dog run, and boy, what a mess. I think Inca, who we call Inca-Stinka, found some chili or something, maybe someone in the house threw something out to make sure Gramps didn't get it!

The problem with it all was that I wasn't able to just shovel the doll heads and all into the trashcan. Mom wanted me to 'retrieve' them in case Aggie wanted to put them back on the dolls' bodies. That is so disgusting. Let me break this point down.

Can you imagine some little girl coming over to the house and Mom saying, "Oh, Aggie, get out your dolls," and the little girl is playing with them and she is all happy and everything and she kisses her little dollies like little girls do. They were all in a bunch of dog poop! Isn't anyone going to say that to the mom? What I am saying is why did I have to retrieve these things. It didn't matter; I still had to put them in a bag—yeah. Thank God I had gloves and boots.

The thing that gets me is it's not like Aggie's room is even on this side of the house. Why didn't she just throw them out her own side? I think she might have thought they would be disguised in this dog-stuff or something. I definitely think after this one, she needs to start attending those *special* after school meetings with a *special* doctor. Yeah, that is what she definitely needs to do.

Well, I was on the side yard when I heard Big Bro Nitwit banging around his trashcans. He was picking them up, rolling them around, standing back and gazing at them. It sure was strange. You know why? He had a girl's dress with him, yeah, weird. It wasn't on him, but still, a dress? He also had roller-skates, a couple of mops, and a bag of some sort. It looked like the little paisley zipper bags my sisters have in their bathroom.

At first I thought, cool—he's making some kind of robot, so every fourth or fifth doll head I plopped into the old trash bag hanging in our trashcan, I'd look up to see Big Bro Nitwit's progress. He wasn't going very quickly. I think the only thing he had done in forty-five minutes was select the right trashcan for his robot . . . and he was staring at it, just staring at it.

I went back to the doll heads. Aggie must have thrown 100 here. I started doing the flick with the shovel, trying to arc the heads into the can, but the dog-wash was getting on me and that made more work and the heads were really planting themselves like unexploded grenades into the doggie piles.

I looked over at Big Bro Nitwit. He was now using Elmer's glue to attach the roller-skates to the bottom of the trashcan. That was never going to work. He needed help; he needed my help and really: Your sister's doll heads in poop or a robot! Okay, if you are throwing the heads into the poop, but not picking them up . . . and saving them. What was my mom thinking? Beheaded poop-caked doll heads? That's just nuts.

I chose robot. I went over to Big Bro Nitwit. I figured I am pretty good at stuff like trashcan robots. They're made outside or in the garage and that's where all my chores are,

21

except for the putting away of the dishes, and my own laundry, and now I have to clean Gramps' bathroom. I swear we have too many bathrooms, but Dad put in an extra one for Gramps. You know—burritos and all! It hasn't helped, but the vent is right under my sister Cece's window—haha.

So I wanted to help Big Bro Nitwit. I wanted to get out of the dog run. I hate the dog run. We didn't used to have one. We have the woods right in the backyard. Not right *in* the backyard—we have like an acre with a bunch of grass, a pool, and a horseshoe pit before the woods, but we have the woods and Inca and Casey used to go there and do their business. The woods are like a reserve or something, so it's all nature stuff. The dogs are natural, but I will say, the stuff they make doesn't seem that natural, pee-yew!!! Especially when doll heads are all in it—that is not natural on so many levels. Aggie is going to pay and the Nitwits should pay too. It is their fault that we even have a dog run. I'll get to that at sometime. It's *crazy*, of course.

I needed to go work on a robot. I grabbed a few things from the shed and headed over to Big Bro Nitwit. He was grunting and sweating and he had cut himself on his leg, but he didn't even seem to mind. This is one thing about all the Nitwits: They are focused. It might not be on the most sensible thing, but they are focused. They get something into their heads and they don't let it go. From Lil' Bro Nitwit to Grandma Nitwit, they stick to it no matter what and I mean no matter what. I think that may be why they don't always get language. They hear or understand a certain meaning of something and they stick to it.

However, it is one reason it's good to join a robot project with a Nitwit—you know it's going to last until the end, until it gets finished. Except this wasn't a robot project.

I wasn't sure at first—Big Bro Nitwit was focused.

I asked, "Do you want me to put those skates on your robot? I've got a socket set here and some bolts."

Big Bro Nitwit kind of grunted, but he moved back, so I moved in. It was pretty easy. The bottom of the trashcan was really thin, and thankfully, Big Bro Nitwit had cleaned it out pretty well. It still smelled; it was a trashcan after all. Oh, and for you folks that have only had plastic trashcans, this one was one of the old metal trashcans, the ones that are in all the cartoons and everything. They make great noises when you bang them. That reminds me of a time we went camping in Yosemite, the national park in California.

We were in some campsites with our tents and someone told my family a story of a bear ripping open the side of a tent and bending down and licking off the cold cream on some lady's face. So being about five years old, I was scared. I didn't use cold cream. I didn't even know what it was. I didn't care. If a bear were going to do that for some makeup, it would do it for anything.

It was dinnertime; the sun was going to be down soon when we suddenly heard all these pots banging. People try to scare bears by banging pots, but all I think it does is scare kids. That's what it did to me. Good reason too, there was a bear. There was a bear and I did the only thing a smart five year old should do. I didn't run into the tent. I didn't hide behind my dad. I didn't climb a tree; bears are great climbers. I ran to the truck, jumped in and locked all the doors. I've seen YouTube—bears can open unlocked doors.

That's when things got really loud. All I could hear is pounding. I thought it was the bear and then I realized the pounding was pounding on both sides of the truck. I finally focused. It was my sisters, Aggie and Cece. They wanted in. I shook my head—no way was I risking opening the door. Are they crazy? There is a bear outside. Don't they know that bears will lick makeup right off your face and open unlocked doors? I just kept shaking my head. I couldn't risk it. It was alright in the end. Let me break it down:

The bear moseyed on over to some romantic couple's campground with their picnic table covered in a red and white checkered cloth and their little plates filled with spaghetti and meatballs and their two candles flickering in the little breeze and their bowl of salad with its croutons and loaf of fancy long bread, and sat down. The couple just backed up. The bear ate everything, even picked up their bottle of wine and gulped it all down. That bear had a great night out at the campsites. I so wish I had a picture.

I think I fell asleep in the truck. I don't remember, but it was the first and only night for that romantic couple. In fact, they left right then. So anyway, those types of trashcans reminded me of how I saved my own life when I was five.

I punched holes through the trashcan, put in the bolts, fed them through the base of the skates, and Big Bro Nitwit had the starts to his rolling robot. I shook my head and smiled. It was a good job.

Big Bro Nitwit started yanking one of the mops apart.

"What are you doing to the mop?" I asked.

"Hair," Big Bro Nitwit said.

"Robots don't have hair," I said.

He grunted and tore at the mops some more. He was making a mess. I didn't understand why a robot would have hair, but Big Bro Nitwit was focused as only Nitwits get focused . . . and Nitwits get focused.

"Why don't you—"

On no! My sister Cece is looking for me. What is it today? Thursday, big laundry day. My sister's stuff was in the washer. I threw it in the dryer. I probably shrunk something of hers—again. Mom will make me earn some money to replace whatever I ruined. It's not even ruined, but they all claim that "It doesn't fit right"; "It doesn't feel right"; "The color has changed." Girls' clothing is stupid!!! Either that or I forgot to take out something of Gramps' or Grandma's. That stuff smells funny. Sometimes you don't smell it for twenty minutes or so—ha—that'd be great, my sisters are out of the house on a date twenty minutes away and Gramp's stink is all over them . . . that's epic.

Oh well, I better go or Cece will make something up and it'll just be worse for me. It's true, I swear, my sisters make up things about me all the time so they get out of doing chores.

I had a razor blade in the tool kit. It made it much easier for Big Bro Nitwit to cut the "hair" for the robot. I didn't say anything else about it, but c'mon, robots do not have hair, cyborgs maybe, mutant alien semi-metallic life forms coming to overtake Earth, yeah, but not your everyday, built in front of the garage, neighborhood trashcan robot. I told Big Bro Nitwit that, but he just grunted.

This robot was going to look stupid with hair! I didn't know at the time but Big—

Oh, Cece is at the door. I didn't "find" her, but Mom saw me, so I better hide in the closet. I can't go out the window. Dad won't let us do that anymore (my sister Aggie!) and anyway Gramps is down there soaking his feet in sea sponges and seaweed. I wonder what Sponge Bob would say about that.

Gramps said that he learned from some midshipman. It's disgusting. He has a tank in the shed, a saltwater one where he raises the sponges, and a bunch of these flat bins with pipes and pumps connecting them all. The shed is pretty big. It's like a garage. The sponge soaking is supposed to be relaxing, the soaking of the feet that is. You sure can learn some interesting things from the guys in the Navy.

I can't go out the window. I have to hide in the closet. I have to hide. Cece sounds, well, she sounds animated! She's knocking on the door like a bear wants her dinner . . . or her for dinner—haha.

I fell asleep in the closet. Whatever Cece wanted, it must have taken care of itself. She wasn't here when I woke up and went to get dinner. I had such a headache. I get such head-aches when I take a nap, especially an unintentional nap.

Well, the next thing with Big Bro Nitwit was crazy. Big Bro Nitwit covered the trashcan with one of his aunt's dresses. Yeah, a robot with a dress! Then he affixed the mop strands to the lid (it was one of those pop-up lids) and colored the lid with all of the junk he had in the girl's bath-room bag. He made a face and put rouge and mascara on it, but it didn't work; it wasn't sticking.

Big Bro Nitwit eventually found some paint. He wasn't making a trashcan robot. He was making a giant, roll-ing, dress wearing, makeup stained, cruddy painted, mop strand-headed trashcan DOLL!!! Can you believe it? He better watch out with Aggie. She might tear the lid off and throw in a heap of dog poo.

I mean, how could he do it? Wasn't he a boy? Wasn't he Big Bro, BIG BRO Nitwit. He was big and a bro. What was happening here?

Then he asked if I would keep the crazy robot for a few days. I didn't say anything and he started taking it to my house. I didn't know what to do. Nobody better see us, me, with this thing! He did ask politely, so I didn't protest. He did say he would pick it up in a couple of days, so I guess I could keep it hidden that long. He mumbled something about his family that I didn't quite catch, but I think he was worried that they would play with it or something, so I allowed him to roll it to the shed. He did a little pirouette with it a couple of times, spinning like a madman. I figured, okay, my sisters never go to the shed and they're the only ones that would put up a stink about it. I thought it would be alright. It was better then alright when everything was done. Hehehehe, actually it's epic.

Well, wouldn't you know, Big Bro Nitwit came over that Friday all dressed up and took the trashcan robot doll thing, put it in his parents' car and drove off with it.

About an hour later, my sisters Trudy and Cece came home with one crazy story, crazier than their ripped and stained dresses. Yeah, they had ripped and stained dresses, but what happened to them was nothing compared to the crazy stuff that happened with Big Bro Nitwit.

Big Bro Nitwit brought the trashcan robot doll thing to St. Hub's. He brought it right into the gym and, when the music started, he started dancing with it. Yeah, his mop-top, dress wearing, roller-skating, (my bolts in the roller-skates really held up—for awhile) multi-painted trashcan robot doll was his dance partner. Oh, I wish I could have seen that—how crazy.

No one went near him though, but that didn't keep him from getting near everyone else. He was swinging his partner around like he had roller-skates on too. Then, when my sisters weren't paying attention to what was surely an awesome spectacle, Trudy's dress was caught by a barb on the side of the robot dance partner as Big Bro Nitwit spun it around and it tore her dress right in the behind region and she screamed and grabbed Cece who had two cups of punch and spilled them all over herself and Trudy and, then when Trudy grabbed Cece to go to the bathroom, she slipped in the puddle and tore Cece's dress in the behind region knocking them into the refreshment stand that tumbled more punch and cupcakes with three inch frosting and gumdrops and gummy bears all over them. High school dances sound great.

I guess everyone was concentrating on my sisters and they didn't realize that Big Bro Nitwit had started everything, so he kept on going. I have other sources that told me what happened when my sisters were in the bathroom. Big Bro Nitwit just kept dancing like a maniac with his trashcan doll dance partner.

The trashcan really smelled, my sisters said. I don't remember it being that bad, but then again, we were outside when we were working on it. They said that the whole place stunk and eventually something started leaking from the trashcan.

When my sister Cece came out of the bathroom, all stained and torn, one of the teachers finally told Big Bro Nitwit: "You need to take the trashcan out."

"That's what I am doing," said Big Bro Nitwit and kept dancing and dancing fast, and then one of the skates fell off (Hey, not my fault; that is the trashcan's fault, the metal was so thin on the bottom, and I didn't know he was going to be so violent with it), and this stuff was being flung all over the floor and people were slipping in it, not my sisters, though. I think this is why they weren't so mortified about their stained and torn dresses when they came home because so many other people were slipping in the smelly stuff and getting different kinds of stains while Trudy and Cece avoided the nasty part of Big Bro Nitwit's trashcan fling fest.

The teacher, I think it was Mr. McSweeney. (He teaches history and coaches track at St. Hub's. They have a really good track team there. Of course my sisters don't run track. Trudy is in the plays—she's okay. Cece plays volleyball—it's so Cece and it's fine, and she's a French kisser. I have a postcard, well her postcard, to prove it. Aggie cheers at football games—that's cool . . . the football games.)

As Big Bro Nitwit kept spinning his trashcan date and things were flying all over the gym, Mr. McSweeney shouted, "What do you mean?"

Guess; go ahead and give it a shot. Here it is.

This is what my sisters said Big Bro Nitwit said: "My mom told me that it was about time I take at least one of the garbage cans out . . . so here I am . . . taking this one out. She looks nice, doesn't she?"

These Nitwits, are they great or what?

Boy, my sisters said that trashcan stunk and so many people slipped and tripped and fell in and over whatever was falling out of it.

"It was disgusting—"

"It was like sludge—"

"It was lumpy sludge and—"

"And there were hairy lumps."

"Hairy," I whispered. I had a thought. Can you guess it? I bet you can guess this one. I was thinking hairy, stinky, sludgy lumps from a trashcan that was in our shed. I looked out at the dog run. Where was that old plastic bag of dog dirty doll heads I had to save? Yep, you guessed it.

Let me break it down for you. I went to the shed. Gramps must have moved the bag. That's my theory. Gramps must have gone in there for his sponges and wanted our trashcan for something and simply moved the bag into Big Bro Nitwit's can. He must have dumped the bag over. I hadn't tied it off or anything. Then, Big Bro Nitwit, focused on his goal, simply put the trashcan in his car and brought it to school.

At the dance my sisters couldn't avoid Big Bro Nitwit's crazy dancing and one thing led to another. The super spinning must have torn holes in the bottom of the trashcan that was super thin from all the wet stinky goopy gunk that had been dumped into it over the years. So when Big Bro Nitwit starting going wild, he just shook up the contents and it started seeping out. Once one of the skates broke free making a hole big enough, the end was near, and it was doggie-poo doll heads all over the place.

Crazy, huh?

Now Big Bro Nitwit has Saturday detention—forever.

Well, once again, if you are ever asked, "Why did Big Bro Nitwit take a trashcan to a dance?"

His mom told him to take the garbage out.

4

GET! GET! GET!

I've heard of guests and fish stink after three days—and I get it, and I certainly know one Nitwit, a robot doll, and a dance can make it stink. I think you all get that. But back to the fish, a fish sitting out after three days almost smells as bad as that dead cat my friend Beep found and brought over in a wagon. That was so bad and so cool. You have to know what to do with a dead cat. That is really important, especially when you have annoying sisters.

So guests stink, like they don't put down the toilet seat or they cut their toenails on the living room couch (Brent and Grandma do that) or eat the last dozen cookies. Grandma also pours things down my sisters' toilets, and they go crazy like it's some cardinal sin or act of war or something, but then Grandma just tunes them out and cuts her nails or eats a dozen cookies (She says, "I cook 'em; I can eat 'em" — Grandma!) while watching some crime show.

Mom won't let her watch any cooking shows, because Grandma always cries when they cook fish. She can't watch the detective show *Monk*, either. Remember I told you I got into trouble for joking about monkfish. I think it has something to do about that and that that *Monk* show is on all the time. (Yeah, three that's in one sentence!)

Oh, and the cookies that guests would eat and Grandma does eat are real good cookies, real good, and she will eat them, but I guess guests do a whole bunch of other things that kind of ruin your routine. They wake up at 5:30 and turn on the Weather Channel at 35 volume or sleep late and force you to sneak around or they use all the hot water or they borrow a car and leave wet burger wrappers in it and don't fill up the tank. I'll tell you this: It was like Grandpa Nitwit yelling at the trees in his yard for a week.

Yep, he yelled at the Nitwit family trees for a whole week. He yelled all through the day, yelling and yelling and yelling with some brief stops. I'll get to that.

It doesn't really snow here in winter. It gets cold, real cold, and we get ice storms, and once in awhile some pretty flakes flutter down, but it's still a real winter; we have seasons, and everything pretty much goes as it should: Birds take off; animals go sleeping; grandparents go to Florida, except mine and the Nitwits; Trudy will slide Mom's car into a parked car and then another one and then another one and then do it again a couple of days later and then Cece will do it. I'm never going to get to drive when I get older—there will be no cars allowed on my street! Sisters . . . uhhhhh!

So I was outside on the first day that Grandpa Nitwit started his yelling and I mean yelling. My mom wanted to go to the store, but it had been so cold, I had to warm up her battery with a portable heater to make it work. Of course she had left the car outside instead of pulling it in the garage. I told her, but she wouldn't let me drive it into the garage, and she *nicely* said that none of my sisters needed to bother. Yeah, we all can see through that one—crash, bang, boom!

One time I tried to move Dad's car when I wanted to play some basketball. Well, we have the slightest slope on the driveway and I wasn't sitting in the car when I released the emergency brake, and the car rolled right back into the street. It rolled back and forth like a really slow skateboarder on a flattened half-pipe. I finally was able to park it on the street. Dad never said anything about his car not being in the driveway, but Trudy did. That was a tough weekend!

So Grandpa Nitwit just started yelling. Boy was he yelling. I thought that their house was on fire or a wolverine had bit his butt. Whatever, it was sure alarming.

I snapped a photo. It's in that box somewhere. At first I didn't know what he was saying or to whom he was saying it, and then I edged a little closer. I heard him, and even though he was looking up at the sky, I thought he was yelling at me because he yelled, "Get out of here! Go! Get Going! Get out of here! Get! Get! Get!"

So I did.

I went inside; told my sisters, but they didn't care or do anything. They just asked if the car was warm. I forgot to hook it up. I had to go back outside. It was freezing. It was one of those cold days that if you stick your tongue to a pole it would freeze, and of course, across the street, there were Big Bro Nitwit and Lil' Bro Nitwit and Big Sis Nitwit and Aunt Nitwit and Grandpa Nitwit. Guess what they were doing; go ahead guess. Here it is: They were all standing around their flagpole with their tongues stuck to it. I have a great picture of that too; I think it's down in the basement. Well, at least Grandpa Nitwit wasn't yelling anymore. I walked—

Oh, Eddie is at my window. He is such a good climber.

Real quick, on Wednesday Eddie found his own dead animal—well not the whole thing. It was, is, a piece of an animal. It's a rabbit leg. He said it was right there on a path near a creek to the Monkey. It was there like the bobcat that had been munching it dropped it or was full or something. It was fresh, like red-fresh if you get what I am saying. Of course Eddie picked it up and took it home.

He said, "Hey, a rabbit's foot is good luck."

I looked at the not so fresh leg! There was a heck of a lot more than a foot. "Not for the rabbit," I said.

Beep now has a dead cat and Eddie has a fresh rabbit's foot—cool. I've got a trashcan of doggie-poo doll heads. It's back in the shed. Yeah, Mom wanted me to get those things back! They are there and I haven't said a word about them.

So I heard Grandpa Nitwit three straight days. It was so cold. The trees were so bare. The street was so slick. The ground was so hard. The air was so cold it burned. Three days straight I heard him, but every afternoon silence. Yeah, all the Nitwits were at the pole, tongues attached. I went over the first day with some water. They all started growling waving their arms. Lil' Bro Nitwit was kicking. I thought they were happy to have me release them from the frozen pole. I was wrong, but I didn't know. I gently measured and poured water on Aunt Nitwit's tongue and you know what she did. You want to guess. I bet you don't get this one. Here it is: She punched me in the face. Yeah, she punched me in the face and the water went flying, almost turning to hail as I tumbled over in pain. What, the ground was hard, real hard.

First, I wasn't even up on my feet yet, when Aunt Nitwit was in my face screaming, "I lost. You made me lose."

I rubbed my nose. Aunt Nitwit scrambled back to her spot and slopped her tongue back on the pole. There was a terrible barrage of grunts and growls, shoving and kicking. I think the other Nitwits were protesting Aunt Nitwit's reattachment.

I left as fast as I could. The punch wasn't that hard. Let me break it down: She did have on padded ski gloves. It was

37

more of a glance. It just shocked me. It was a sucker punch. I told Brent. 'Yeah, you're a sucker' is all he said. 'Punched to the ground by an old lady.' I don't know why I talk to him at all. It still was crazy being punched by Aunt Nitwit.

Uh, my sisters refused to put the car in the garage. They are so lazy. I just know that they were scared. I had even spent an afternoon, on Christmas vacation, cleaning a spot for the car. I had to move all of Grandma's old clothing and some old school projects and some summer stuff and put it in the crawl space above the garage. I looked for old signed baseballs and treasure maps but I didn't find any. I did find what I think is a picture of my Dad when he was around my age. He had giant ears. Oh, I can't wait to bring this thing out some day when more of the family is over. It will be a riot. He had no teeth either. He fell off his bike or something, if I remember right. He looks like an alien or a zombie or an alien zombie. I need to find that picture. It's around here somewhere, probably in my underwear drawer. My sisters will never look in there for anything! I probably have more junk in there than underwear now. I better clean it out. Brent would look in there and he—he tends to look for things all the time . . . well, when he is here, and he's always here in the middle of the night, so it would be real easy for him to have a look without my protesting—I sleep deep.

So finally, like after a week, the police came down the street to the Nitwits' house. It was a Friday. I didn't have any chores and I was trying to make a frozen dirt birdbath. I was taking the dirt and—

Cece just went berserk. It's hilarious. Eddie left his lucky half a rabbit's leg in my room and, when Cece came in to get me to help with moving something in the garage, (my sisters are all like that, when they want help with something that isn't Mom or Dad approved, they get all nice to me) she saw the leg o' rabbit on my nightstand. She screamed like crazy. It even made Gramps come up the stairs, but when he saw what it was, he grabbed it and simply laughed as he went back down stairs. Cece was nowhere. I guess it wasn't that important, and let me just say that Eddie no longer has his lucky rabbit's foot.

Well, it must have been an hour I was outside in the cold. I like outside cold because then it's hot chocolate and I am all over outside hot chocolate, the steam, the burning cup, the chocolaty goodness—ahhhh. So I am out there an hour and I hear Grandpa Nitwit go to town yelling up into the sky. "Get out of here! Go! Get Going! Get out of here! Get! Get! Get!"

The police rolled up to him, and I sneaked over to hear what they were saying.

You know how I told you that guests and fish stink after three days (never mind dead cats). Well, Grandpa Nitwit was *upset* with all the trees. Yes, you read it right. He was *upset* with all the trees. He said to Officer Hawkins that he was yelling at them to go away.

"It's motivation," said Grandpa Nitwit.

"Motivation for what?" asked Officer Hawkins. "I know it is good to talk to your plants, but to yell at them. Now . . . "

Grandpa Nitwit looked perturbed like Officer Hawkins should know. Grandpa Nitwit turned toward the tree and yelled, "Get out of here. Get. Get. Get." He turned back to Officer Hawkins. Officer Hawkins gave a 'I-don't-know' shrug.

You want to guess what Grandpa Nitwit said next. Go ahead and guess. Maybe one of you will get it, but I doubt it. Only he, and Officer Hawkins and his pretty partner Officer Carino . . . what, she's pretty, she is. Only they and I know. We all know that Grandpa Nitwit said in the cold of winter:

"I want them to leave." He tapped at his head. "It's reverse psychology."

The officers just shook their heads.

"Pretty, pretty leaves, so nice and pretty," said Grandpa Nitwit looking up to the barren limbs.

I can see some trees out my window. They are nice and all, but c'mon.

Well, that is what Grandpa Nitwit said and that is why he was yelling. So if you're ever asked, "Why did Grandpa Nitwit spend a week yelling at his trees?"

He wanted them to leave. It was reverse psychology . . . or more like Nitwit psychology.

5

THE 'S' WORD

"Ticks suck!"

I can say that and not get in trouble. Mom doesn't like the 's' word. I even used to say, when I was younger and I didn't like something at school, that it was the worst 's' word in the world! I'd come home and say something about cutting triangles and pasting them for an hour that it was the 's' word. My sisters still remind me of that one, but in fact, I still say it sometimes, sort of a habit.

My friends get into it too. "That's so the 's' word," Beep and Eddie will say and laugh, but they were there when I was younger and they know where it comes from, so it's not so bad, and Beep says *beep* after all. The truth is, though, that ticks suck and I can say that because ticks suck like a vacuum. I have proof.

See Beep and Eddie were over, and this kid a street over, Fernando, he was there with us, and I don't know how it started, but after it did, Big Sis Nitwit and Big Bro Nitwit came over too. This is when I definitely found out that ticks suck and Nitwits are way crazy.

See, our yards are real big and, in the front at my house, we have a pebbled walkway, with a billion pebbles but also with some good-sized river rocks, those smooth almost flat ones. The walkway goes from a bench to the side of the house. It is a good twenty feet so there are a ton of pebbles.

Well, we started for some reason to, not throw as Mom said it later, but to skip the pebbles off each others' heads.

It didn't hurt—at first.

We actually moved our heads to butt the pebbles. It was to see how high we could send one or how far we could skip one off our heads. I don't remember when Big Sis Nitwit and Big Bro Nitwit came over, but they joined in. Only thing Big Sis Nitwit seemed to do was get the rocks slimy when she finally took her finger out of her nose to pick one up and throw it at her brother.

Okay, the finger wasn't permanently there, but it was there a lot and it has to do with everything. It shows you just how crazy—

Oh, no, Dad just found my science experiment and I don't think he will be happy. See, I wanted one of my sisters to find it, and I was going to record her reaction. It is kind of like a biological response thing. I wanted, hopefully, to get the heart rate and the facial expressions and see how long until Aggie, Cece, or Trudy said she wanted to kill me or tell Mom we can at least send him to Timbuktu, but Dad found it. Why is he even home now?

I think he knows it's mine. Well, I'm borrowing it. It's not mine. You want to guess what it is. I'll give you a hint. It's Beep's. I bet some of you know. That's right—Beep dug up the cat, and I put it in my sisters' bathroom. It doesn't really smell, the cat, the bathroom, yeah—sisters . . . uhh-hhh! The cat doesn't smell unless you stick it right up to your nose and give a good sniff. The weirdest thing is how stiff and flat it is. I don't know, maybe Dad will blame Grandma or Aunt Jess. I should have put it in the toilet; then Grandma for sure would get blamed. I'd still take the rap—Grandma's cookies are too good and I just can't make them like she can—and it wouldn't be right and I would just beat myself up over it. What's Dad doing home?

I have to clean my sisters' bathroom now for a month and not tell them why (Dad doesn't want to have to remodel the whole thing) and Beep isn't allowed over for a week, but he can come over to get his cat. Dad told me to throw it away, but it's not mine I argued. I had to return it to Beep. I guess that's it—I'll take it, not the best idea, but now I need a new science project.

Well, Big Sis Nitwit was busy with a pebble of her own, one up her nose, and she wouldn't move her head and Big Bro Nitwit kept getting bigger pebbles to throw at her and she kept getting hit. The rest of us were still skipping the small pebbles off of each other's skulls. That is when Beep told me I had one stuck in my ear.

"No I don't," I said.

"Yeah you do."

"No"

"Yeah."

"No!" I said.

"Yeah! What the beep, you do."

"No!!"

"Yeah!!!"

"NNNNOOOOOOOOOOOOO!!!!!!!"

"It's totally beep in there."

"Nothing hit my ear."

"You sure?"

"It's there, a little black one," said Fernando. He had crept closer to investigate.

"But nothing hit my ear! Nothing at all!" I was getting mad.

It did feel strange though. Maybe it was because everyone was talking about it. Now that I thought about it, it had felt weird since the night before when I woke up in the pile of leaves in the front of the house at 9:00 or so.

Man, everyone was staring at my ear.

"Yep," they all said. "You got a rock in your ear."

44

"It sucked." I'm allowed to say that because it wasn't a rock, it was a tick! and that is what ticks do—suck!

"Trying to suck all your brains out?" said Doctor Glad. Yeah, that is his name and he always says, '*Glad* to see you' and '*Glad* you're being healthy' and 'I'll be *Glad* not to see you for this again' and a hundred other *Glad* sayings. He has them plastered all over his office walls. Of course my sister Trudy was with us and she said, "What brains?" She says that all the time. She used to put her hand on my head and wiggle it and say, "This is a brain sucker; what is it doing? Starving." She'd laugh like Gramps' laugh, kind of freaky now that I think about it. She still does it! Boy, am I'm glad I have Beep's cat back. It's in the shed, in the wall, behind some tarpaper.

So ticks suck. They suck blood, my blood. Ticks suck! And since Doctor Glad even said it, and I'm sure my mom would love me to grow up to be a doctor, I can say it. "Ticks SUCK!" She says it to me all the time, not about ticks but about being a doctor.

So I went to the doctor, but so did Big Sis Nitwit. See, she was digging for a boulder of her own in her left nostril, and Big Bro Nitwit picked up a pretty good sized rock, a smooth river rock, smooth and heavy. This was no pebble. He threw it at his sister. It didn't hit her head. It didn't whistle by; it didn't break a window. It smashed right into Big Sis Nitwit's nose. It probably would have been worse had her finger not been there.

We all heard a crack, and once she took her finger out, we all saw the blood. We all saw and heard Big Sis Nitwit jump up and cheer. She cheered—she was happy. You know why. You want to guess why. Go ahead and try to guess this one. Well, here it is.

"Why are you cheering?" I asked.

"I'm happy," Big Sis Nitwit said sounding like she had a double cold.

"Why?" I repeated.

"I get to have rhinoplasty," Big Sis Nitwit said.

"Rhinoplasty?" said Beep.

"Yeah, a nose job, I get a new nose," said Big Sis Nitwit.

"So?" said Fernando.

"So it will be the first time in my life that no one will make fun of me for picking my nose!"

I wonder if my doctor would be *glad* about that.

Big Sis Nitwit skipped back home, blood dripping all over her shirt, to share the good news—Nitwits!

It makes me want to blow my nose. I have to go get some tissues.

Oh well, there it is. If you are ever asked, "Why did Big Sis Nitwit smile when her brother hit her in the face with a rock?"

She got to pick her nose.

6

FLIPPIN' BURGERS

I was about to tell you something else about the Nitwits, but I had to clean out Gramps' room. There will be no kiss tonight. I have to come up with a better plan. It is not going to be so straightforward. My sisters are all busy. Gramps fell asleep with, well, guess what he was doing. You'll never guess. I'll give you a hint: It has to do with sea sponges. Here it is. Gramps was soaking his feet in a sponge bath. Get it—he gives his feet a sponge bath. I don't think it's the sponge bath people probably did in the Navy or Marines or Special Ops. I've had a sponge bath with a washcloth—a real quick 'poor man's' bath my mom calls it. It is one of those quick ones after a late night and then a real hectic morning when everyone gets up groggy and has to get going with no time to wash your hair. My sisters complain so much about those types of mornings. It's so worth it.

47

Anyway, Gramps brought the hose into his room to fill his tub and he fell asleep while soaking his feet in his tub, and I don't know when he fell asleep, but there was water everywhere. It all reminds me of a story that happened before I was born.

It seems my sisters (Trudy and Cece) decided to have a fight with each other in their playpen and their weapons of choice were whatever they could grab, but after the stuffed animals went over the side and the blankies and binkies, all they had left was what they were wearing and the only thing the two of them were wearing was their diapers . . . and what was in them.

Dad brought the hose into the house for the walls and the ceiling and the floor and everything else. Mom immediately switched their food to stuff with less fiber. I think it is the reason I had to eat a ton of bananas when I was little.

So I just finished squeegeeing, (that is a word, I think) Gramps' floor. I am so glad there is hardwood and tile downstairs. I am so glad we caught the water before it went into the basement—carpet down there. I haven't checked though. I better check the basement.

It did; the water went down there, but it wasn't much. I dried it up with towels from the bin. It came down a wall. They weren't Gramps', the towels that is, thank God, but they were Grandma's. It smells down there. I don't think any air-hockey is in order for a few days.

What a mess; let me break it down: First off, Gramps wanted his feet soaked. He didn't want to be in the shed. He said it kind of smelled. *He* said it smelled! Well, he brought in the tub. He must have been real relaxed and fell asleep—makes sense. On the other hand, with my sisters, they were babies; the hose, my dad freaked. That's it. Dad had no idea what to do. The Nitwits, haven't gotten to them, so here it is:

The Nitwits had stopped by our house after a week or two from moving in. They brought over a pot roast. Want to guess. Go ahead. Here it is and here they went again. It was a really hot pot, yeah a pot, roasted on their grill—a pot roast . . . Nitwits!

Mom just said thanks and asked them to dinner, but since it was morning and they hadn't had lunch, they all sniggered and left.

Big Bro Nitwit had said to me: "Dinner at eleven in the morning? You guys are weird."

'We're weird,' I said to myself. I just knew that if I said it out loud something would go wrong. I said more to myself, 'You guys just brought over a pot roast at eleven in the morning and it's a pot . . . roasted!!!' Nitwits!

Well, I didn't bother to tell him that Mom was telling them to come back at dinnertime. This was one of the first times my folks met the Nitwits and my mom just did that 'oh-smile' and said okay. What else can you do with a *roasted* pot.

Soon after, we were invited to the Nitwits' house for a backyard meal—of course they meant immediately. I guess they were really hungry. They obviously weren't getting fat on pot roast!

I think they had started to eat, and then came over and Mom Nitwit said, "We'd like to invite you over for lunch."

"Sounds nice, when?" asked my dad.

"Well, right now of course. It is lunch time." They sniggered.

"Right, right," Dad said.

They waited.

Dad wanted to be neighborly, so he collected whoever was home and we went over to the Nitwits' backyard.

It was a nice thing to do on a sleepy Saturday, but oh, the food.

First, they had a three-bean salad. Gramps went right for it. We didn't know it was a three-bean salad. Gramps' just picked up the bowl and went to a chair under and tree and started eating . . . and laughing. We didn't know what he had. It looked like a bunch of green lettuce, and it was, but there was a bunch of beans on the bottom. Gramps has a nose for beans, but apparently not for their result! I know you think that the Nitwits would only have three beans in their three bean salad, three individual beans, but Big Sis Nitwit said they were going to do that, but they thought cans of beans come with so many more beans and three beans wouldn't feed many people so they dumped all three cans of beans in with the lettuce . . . duh! Three bean salad!

The potato salad, you guessed it, the same thing, a bunch of green lettuce with a couple of potatoes plopped on top. I don't even think the potatoes were cooked.

The hotdogs—yeah—no—they didn't have any canines, but Dad Nitwit did ask us about our dogs and how would we prepare them, you know, if we wanted our own *hotdogs*. The dog run went up the next day—yeah, that's the story of the dog run. Here is a quick break down: Dad was a little freaked out by Dad Nitwit and especially his grin when he asked about Inca and Casey; Dad Nitwit looked much too much like a cattle wrestler dusting off his chaps with his hat after a fourteen hour drive, eyeing some grilled prairie critter, and telling the cook he'd like two *helpin's*—rare!

The Nitwits did have hamburgers and, yes, they were made out of . . . ham. They fell apart like crazy, but what was—

Oh brother, Brent just came in here. I told you he does this, but most of the time it's at night. He is looking for something. He says that it is really important, but he won't tell me what it is. Maybe it's another poem from *Chickens Don't Have Fingers*. I'll get to that later. (I hope I get to all the I'll-get-back-to-that-later stuff. If not, there is so much more about the Nitwits to tell you, and there is always something to plan against my sisters—sisters . . . uhhhhh, that I'm sure I can fill another book or ten.) Brent is rummaging around in my closet. He better not get into my underwear! Beep and Eddie are going to crack up when they read that line by itself: "He better not get into my underwear." That is funny. You know I mean the drawer . . . I hope you know that.

"What do you want?"

51

He didn't respond. He can be real annoying and not respond.

I wish I were bigger. I'd make him respond like the way he makes me. He sits on me and rubs noogies into my head. 'Time for a Monkey–Scrub,' he yells. He hasn't done it in awhile, thank God. He got in trouble when he did a loogie-noogie, otherwise known as a *wet* monkey-scrub. It was disgusting. I think he had been saving up all that throat gunk for a month. He probably would have gotten away with it, but Trudy saw it and I think she wanted to get him back for something. They are always at it. I don't know what it was, so I can't tell you. I'll try to find out about it and, if it is any good, I'll tell you.

Man, if I were bigger . . . I don't like that he comes in here and does this.

"Got it!"

I have no idea what he got, but he's gonna get it one of these days. You know what I mean—I'm still growing; he's pretty much done.

So Mom made us eat or at least try all the food that was offered at the Nitwits. I think that moms sometimes are too nice, too many of those 'oh!-smiles' and 'Yes, thank you's.' The *ham*-burgers were, well, they were awful. It wasn't the ham itself, but it was everything else that we had to pick out: the chunks of charcoal, the twigs, the grass, the bugs, the everything.

See Uncle Nitwit was instructing Big Bro Nitwit about how to cook the burgers and Uncle Nitwit said you only have to flip them once.

"The key to a really good hamburger on the grill is to only flip it once," said Uncle Nitwit.

"Only once," said Big Bro Nitwit concentrating on his task. "Only flip it once?"

"That's right, hamburgers on the grill, only flip once."

Want to guess what Big Bro Nitwit did. I bet most of you guess it. Here it is: Big Bro Nitwit stared at the grill for a good thirty seconds. He was focused. He then put on the grill mitts and . . . a little break down first. What Uncle Nitwit meant or maybe not, but what should be done about flipping burgers is that each individual burger only needs to be flipped once. It is like four minutes on each side. Well, these weren't hamburgers—they were *ham*burgers; maybe there was a special technique. Uncle Nitwit told Big Bro Nitwit that it was time to flip the burgers, so Big Bro Nitwit did, all at once. Yep, he flipped over the entire grill right onto its dome top. Nitwits!

All the coals and the grill were on top of the *ham*burgers and the stuff was so hot Big Bro Nitwit dumped everything on the grass before serving it. Mom made us be good guests and take some onto our plates—crazy. If you're not going to eat it, what is the point? I need to go eat something. I hope Grandma baked something today.

Well, if you're ever asked, "Why did Big Bro Nitwit turn over the whole grill?"

His uncle told him it was time to flip the burgers, so he did, all at once.

7

PLAYIN' BALL

I have a headache right now. It is one of those ones that circles my whole head. It aches, but I wanted to get this one story down about the Nitwits while I'm thinking about it. The kissing plan needs work. I don't know how it is going to happen. I have to get Brent to help me.

Okay, so I was over at the Nitwits' house, in their basement, and I found all these signs. They were signs for businesses, the type of signs that hang over the front door or the front window of a store. They were all signs from businesses that Grandma Nitwit used to run. She sure ran a lot of them.

Big Bro Nitwit said Grandma Nitwit would have a business for a couple of months or something and then start a new one. She had so many signs. I think the moms and grandmas—I say the moms and grandmas because they seem to read to the kids more than the dads and granddads, so I think, well, if dads and granddads read this too, that they would, with the moms and grandmas, get these better than I do. See I don't know what the businesses are so the names just seem confusing to me.

I found one sign that said *Cold Sweat*. Big Bro Nitwit said it was a store that sold iceboxes and saunas. Okay, I got it once I knew what she sold. Big Bro Nitwit said that it was a good business. Another sign was *Fast and Loose*. Big Bro Nitwit said it was Grandma's business of dietician and yoga instructor. I guess it makes sense, but I'm not sure what most of the "original" meanings are supposed to have, and Big Bro Nitwit didn't even know they had "original" meanings, but I've heard some of these sayings before.

There must have been fifty signs here. I don't know why. There were so many there. I should get a list for my parents. They would probably get what each means. Oh, here is another one: *Touch Down*. You know what the original meaning is I'm sure. Want to guess what the businesses were; go ahead. Here it is. It was a petting zoo and a pillow/comforter store. Down pillows are the best. I have one that I've had for about six years. I can't sleep without it. I never let it out of my room. I mean never. It has been in there for six years, except when we are in the tents or camping and then it is right back in to my room!

I guess that is when he overheard us or something. It was a nice day and we were going to go to the park to play some ball. Lil' Bro Nitwit must have heard us invite his brother. We needed bodies for a decent game. I didn't even know if Big Bro Nitwit could play, but it was the season and I was itchin' to play a little ball. Plus, I wanted to get out of the house.

Someone my mom knew was having a baby, and the baby shower was at our house. My sisters were all geeked for it, and I didn't want to get caught in having to do anything. I remember a bridal shower I was stuck at and I had to dress in a bunch of toilet paper. It was humiliating—my sisters have pictures, and not only was I in a toilet paper dress, I had makeup on, yeah a whole bunch of makeup. My three sisters loved it! It's just cruel to make a boy put on makeup and a toilet paper dress just because someone his mom knows is getting married.

However, I thought it would be interesting to hang around for a bit, because Big Sis Nitwit, Mom Nitwit, Aunt Nitwit, and Grandma Nitwit were invited. Mom didn't want to have a big to-do at the house without inviting over the neighborhood ladies. Guess what they brought over. Go ahead and guess. I bet some of you may already have guessed it; the Nitwit ladies did bring a little soap, a little towel, and a little shower cap for the baby's shower.

I could have stayed, but no matter what else was going to happen there, I didn't want to be around all those ladies pinching my cheeks, telling me how much I've grown. Mrs. Garvin is one always asking me if I had picked a college and a major. What are you going to do when you grow up? I'm eleven! All she cares about is your college and your career. She says it's important to pick your major early and start working toward it; then she yaps about her three sons and their great careers—blah, blah, blah.

My sister Trudy says Mrs. Garvin's youngest son, Paul, is a goofball and yeah he has a job, but it's not like he's the president of a company or something. She says he still plays in a rock band on the weekends or just hangs out with his friends at Monkey Lanes Bowling Alley. It's really called Monkey Lanes. There's a logo with a crazy monkey peeling a banana with a bowling pin inside of it. It's a million years old. Back to Paul, I think he was cited one time over in the Monkey for being um, for having lost his swimsuit, if you know what I'm saying. He was naked as a jaybird, yeah, skinny-dippin' in the Monkey. He doesn't sound so grown up, unless that is what grownups do!

Anyway, a baby shower, I didn't want to be there so I took my gear to the park and we started warming up and along comes—

Oh no, Grandma has lost her medicine again. I don't know why I have to look for it in her room every time she loses it. It's not an outside chore, but I am the one that has to crawl around under her bed and nightstands for a pill.

It's disgusting. There are these weird balls of stuff in her sheets and on the floor. I don't know what they are, but I'm going to examine one. I think it could be my science project. They are disgusting—perfect. I don't know why she takes the pills in bed and why if she drops one she simply doesn't get another, pshaw. Whatever, now it is my job. You should—

"Coming." I've gotta go.

Where was I, yeah, the park, but first Grandma's room. I found the pill. It wasn't easy . . . it never is. Here is the break down: She has so much cra— stuff in there. I'm not allowed to say that other word. I think Grandma has everything from the day she was born in 1929 in there. It is like a time-warp gift shop. In there is every letter, every knick knack, every picture, every recipe, every shoe, every doily. . . . She has a million doilies and she never washes them. They are so dusty and hairy. Yes hairy, and that is what I found are those ball things. Mom calls them dust bunnies but they don't hop anywhere; they just sit there and then suddenly move with a tiny wisp of a breath or an opening of a door or a poltergeist dancing. This is when they should be called dust spiders or spider balls. They are like hairy balls of spider webs and head hair and lint or something that can move in any direction when you least expect it. With their eight hairy linty legs they can and will, when you are just about to fall asleep and your eyes are heavy and you are all comfortable and safe, crawl right down your neck into your shirt and down to your back. Grandma has them everywhere.

The worst part is she never cleans her floor. She drops all these circular tissue pads she rubs on herself, and torn wrappers from these little candies, and dirty socks she wears outside, and everything else right on her floor. It's a total hairy horror show. The hardwood looks like carpet.

I don't know how Mom lets her get away with it. I do know Grandma goes crazy if anyone touches anything of hers and maybe that is where it all lies. I think Mom broke something, probably a singing monkfish plaque or something, and Grandma got all upset and wouldn't let her in the room.

Well, it felt like it took about twenty minutes. I hate to say it, but I had to do it in order to see under the bed. I had to—well, I had to—I had to get out of there. For one, it stunk, that weird sick bleach smell, but two, Grandma stares at me—it's creepy. She never takes her eyes off of me, like I'm a thief or something. (I did take one of the dusty hairy spider balls—totally my science project.)

Now, Grandma won't move or help or say anything, so I had to do it—had to do—absolutely had to do what I did. She won't let me wear gloves either. She said 'forensic evidence' one time. She even had some fireplace gloves right there, but I couldn't use them, so I had to do it, and do it barehanded and it wasn't the spider-ball.

I think I might be confusing you. You could guess what I did, but I doubt any of you will get it, maybe a few of you that have a Grandma like mine and chores like mine. Well, here it is: I reached down quickly. It was the only way to do it, and with my bare hands, I had to touch—yes it is true—I can't believe I'm telling you this, but I had to touch my Grandma's girdle. She left it on the floor. She left it in a pile. I couldn't sweep it away with my foot because the pill could have been under it. It wasn't. It was so unnecessary. Ahhhhhhhhhhhhhhhhhhh, Ihadtotouchher*underwear*too!!!!!!!!!!!!!!!!!!!!!!!!!!!

None of it was even necessary. I found the pill, on the nightstand, under a doily—yeah, right on the nightstand!!! It's so unfair. Grandma's a girl; my sisters should have to do this stuff, not me! Sisters . . . uhhhhh.

I'm going outside into the woods and dunking my hand in mud for the next six hours.

Okay, I don't know if Grandma's, um, legacy will ever leave me. I have to talk to Mom about going into that room. You know, I didn't even tell you it's not a room but a whole side of the house, one of the sides that used to be a porch. She has a side of the house for her room and she makes me look all around all the time. I think that my clothes are what clean her floor—my sliding all over looking for stuff sweeps it clean. You could rake me after and get a lint ball the size of a watermelon—that sounds pretty cool—I should see if I can make one. I know just where I would leave it. I'm sure I will have another opportunity; I think she loses her pills on purpose. Yeah, she hides them. I have to make lemonade out of it some how. That is what mom always says. It's not real lemonade. Just wait until Mom says to make lemonade out of a bad situation to the Nitwits. Won't that be a doozey?

So we went to play ball and it was going well and here comes Lil' Bro Nitwit with his Grandfather's cello. That was simply weird to see.

He had it in the black case and was dragging it across the grass. We thought he might want to play a song, *Take Me Out to the Ballgame,* maybe the national anthem, but no, he pulled the cello out and walked right onto the infield with it. Of course we all stopped what we were doing.

"What are you doing?" asked Eddie.

"I brought Grandpa Nitwit's cello," said Lil' Bro Nitwit.

"Yeah?" I said.

"It's a bass, isn't it?"

"I guess," I said.

"It is."

"So what?" said Beep.

"Well, aren't you guys playing baseball? If you are, I am ready to go right after I tune this." He plucked at the strings. "What pitch would you like?"

No one said a word.

I told you about how words get Nitwits like that, but Lil' Bro Nitwit did stop a bunch of grounders, but now that cello is way out of tune. It had a couple of dents in it and a crack on its side. I'm sure it was a good thing Lil' Bro Nitwit couldn't swing it. Man, Big Bro Nitwit though, wouldn't stop talking about baseball. He loved it. He had never played. He went out for the high school team, but what he did—oh, what they all do at school—now that is a whole other—

"Gramps!" My sister Cece is yelling at Gramps. I better go check it out.

Gramps got some fish from Monkey stream. I better hide Grandma's hearing aides or I will be hanging out at the fish shop waiting for that country-ugly monkfish.

I'll get back to more in a bit, but remember if you're ever asked, "Why did Lil' Bro Nitwit bring a cello to the park?"

He wanted to play *base*-ball . . . and he did alright.

8

POSTAL SERVICE

This week has been such a blur. It's not that I have forgotten about the kiss, but I've had tons of homework and the Nitwits—oh the Nitwits. Listen to this one.

We saw her when we drove by on Sunnyslope. We weren't sure at first. We were on our way to get mail at the post office for my aunt. I don't know why it couldn't be delivered to us or why I had to go, but Aunt Jess was all giddy about it and she wanted to pick it up and I still don't know why *I* had to go (no wait, I bet my sisters knew and they complained and offered me up to do it—sisters . . . uhhhhh!), but when we were driving over there, we saw Grandma Nitwit.

She owns her own business in town. In fact, I think I've told you that she has owned a ton of businesses. It seems if they start to do well, she sells them right away. I've told you that she always has these weird combinations selling this and doing that or fixing this and teaching that. I think her husband had a lot of dough, but he isn't around anymore and she likes trying herself out on new fangled ideas and maybe, we thought, it might be one of the those new ideas when we drove by her as she walked down Sunnyslope Street to the post office. It sure was curious and absolutely crazy. She—

Oh brother, Dad just came home and the trashcans aren't out. He's crazy about the trashcans going out . . . Nitwits going out with trashcans—not. We have six of them and they have to be in a certain order. We have three colors: blue, black, and green. I don't know why they have to be in a certain order, and I don't know why they have to be out before sundown, and why they have to be a certain distance from the driveway and a certain distance from the curb, but dad gets like that.

I think he had a toy garbage truck as a kid and he wants the garbage man to have it easy or something . . . or there is some stupid law about it. These are the city plastic ones and not the ones Gramps uses in his shed or the one that Big Bro Nitwit used as his date.

Dad gets like that with all the rules and stuff. He says, 'rules bring simplicity.' Yeah, wouldn't it be simple to simply take out the cans and bring them in, in any order, at any time?

Well, the recycling can is outside the kitchen window, so all we have to do is throw recycling out the window. It's real convenient. So I have to put it there. The garbage cans go to two chutes we have from the second and third floor, so they have to go there. One grass can goes to the back and one next to the garage. So yeah, it makes sense where they go, but on the street, before sundown, I don't know about that. I need to figure that one out.

Well, we were going to the post office. It took forever to find a parking spot and, when we got it, it was a madhouse. The line was easily twenty people, and only two clerks were working the counter. I didn't see why we had to be here at all and why we had to stay when it was going to take so long. I should have brought a game or even a book. My dad always brings a magazine with him wherever he thinks there might be a line. Mom gets mad at him when he reads and she is right there with him. He says it makes it go faster; the line even feels like it rushes him. I totally get it: It's like reading right before school starts and I have a test. I don't have any time to finish. Time just evaporates.

Well, wouldn't you know who walked in fifteen minutes after us, and the only one after us to walk into the post office. It was like we could have saved a quarter of an hour of my life if we left a little later. Guess who it was. Go ahead and guess. Yeah, you got it. It was Grandma Nitwit, but there is no way you know what she was wearing. Guess; go ahead. I know that not one of you knows. There is no way

67

you know. I'm going to tell you what she was wearing. I am. I am going to tell you what she was wearing. It's unbelievable. It's totally crazy. Only a Nitwit would do this. Here it is: She was wearing nothing! That's right, nothing, NOTHING!!!!!!

No way!!! Dad says that the trashcans have to be in a different order. Isn't that nuts. I have to go down there and put them in a different order. I really need to figure this out.

Okay, trashcans done, so Grandma Nitwit. Grandma Nitwit wasn't really wearing nothing, but she wasn't wearing any clothing. I know that sounds weird, but it is the truth. See, she had on or better yet she had stuck to her—stamps. That is right; she was covered in postage stamps, all over, okay, from head to toe, all sorts of stamps: flags, boats, flowers, faces, fireworks, planes. It was a philatelist's dream. (A philatelist is someone who collects stamps.) Then again, it might be a philatelist's nightmare—Grandma Nitwit covered in stamps. Either way, it was crazy.

We finally made it up to the counter, and my Aunt Jess smiled, did a little dance, and asked for her mail. She was given a small bundle. That was it. It wasn't even a package or something cool like a trampoline from some online store. It was simply a bundle of mail. Why was I here?

Aunt Jess jumped up and down like a little kid about to open a birthday present, but she didn't open it right there. She didn't even check through the small rubber banded bundle. She simply motioned for us to go. I really had no idea why I had to be a part of this. Then we were in the car. I was squeezed next to Aunt Jess; Dad drove. My mom was in the back seat on the other side of me. That should have clued me to something, anything. I was the turkey in an old lady sandwich. My mom's not that old but you get the picture. I had no idea what was going on. Well, I soon found out, and I ended up throwing away my shirt as soon as the car hit the driveway.

Aunt Jess was all excited. She wanted to go to the post office for one thing—a postcard. See, some, well, Dad says 'lover' of hers, from way back when, went somewhere and told her he would send a postcard and it would be there by May third. Well, it never came, but she started telling herself that he never said the year and, as May approached, all her hopes were recharged and she had the post office keep her mail because she didn't want anyone in the house to accidentally throw it away—or read it.

I say postcards are fair game. They are right in the open. I remember getting some great ammunition against my sister Cece from a postcard. See, at some camp, she met a boy and he wrote her a postcard from his vacation in Florida and the best part, you'll love this, the best part, I'm laughing right now, it was great, the best part was he wrote that he "wanted to go to France with her again." I didn't know what it meant then, but Aggie told me and HA! what fun that was to hold France over her.

My parents eventually found out that she had been kissing a boy at camp and they were not too happy, but I brought it up as much as possible when Cece was being a bother. I always asked if she and Tom were going to Paris or Calais or Normandy; I looked up a ton of French cities. Oh, and Tom is the name of the boy that wrote the postcard. Cece would get so mad. I had to stop when she threw a book through a window. I didn't do it, so I don't know why I had to stop. I ducked. That's all I did.

So after the post office ride of goo, I threw my shirt away, immediately, right in the trashcan. See, Aunt Jess didn't get her postcard again. She looked through the bundle—nothing there. At first it was a sigh and then a little harrumph and then all I remember is her crying and crying and crying all over my shoulder. That, it turns out, is why I was there . . . a shoulder to cry on . . . and a shirt to goo all over. I think I'd rather have a wet monkey-scrub.

I was so mad at my Mom; she knew exactly what was going to happen. Let me break it down:

Mom just wanted to keep the car clean or something. Man, Aunt Jess is a factory, a super, squirmy, squirty, shooting snot factory, and the factory boilers were all chugging along and the factory doors were wide open. She dug her talons in me and wouldn't let go and gooed all over my shirt, and yes even over the collar, and yes, it was creeping over the shirt and heading for my back when Dad hit the driveway. I tore out of the car, on Mom's side, and tore my shirt off and tossed it into the nearest trashcan—it was green—isn't snot biodegradable.

Dad made me take my shirt out and put it in the black one. Mom made me take it out of the black one and put it in the laundry, but I showed her that I had literally torn it off. I had to pick up some extra chores to pay for a new one. Aunt Jess should have bought me a new one.

I put the shirt back in the green can; the shirt was cotton. I figured that made sense. I headed to the woods. I needed some dirt on me, lots of dirt. I needed mud. I needed to get there. I could feel it on my skin. Some of Aunt Jess's sadness was still on me, was on my skin. I shiver just thinking about it. I made it to the mud, the dirt. It was what I needed. I could soap it off later.

I walked back to the house. I saw Grandma Nitwit; she was covered in a blanket. Later mom told me that she heard Grandma Nitwit as we left the post office tell the mailman that she received a postcard that was stamped 'return to sender' . . . so guess what, go ahead. Here it is, she was . . . returning to sender.

I have to return to the kitchen. Mom made dinner and guess what . . . lots of beans. I know, a crazy dessert ahead of me, but what can I do.

Yeah, so if you are ever asked, "Why did Grandma Nitwit put postage stamps all over herself and walk to the post office?"

She was returning to sender . . . just like the postcard read.

71

9

TRY iT; YOu MiGHT LiKe iT

No one is around tonight, so I'm going to keep writing. I've been a little sick, bronchitis. My plans are on hold again, but it will happen soon. I promise. I mean I've been inside a few days trying not to do anything so I can get rid of this cough, and now TV, YouTube, and video games just don't seem like fun. Well for now, here is a great story; it's one that just shows how crazy the whole group of Nitwits is. You are going to like this one. Uh, it is so bad being in the house that I am thinking about slipping Gramps some chili just so I have an excuse to go outside.

So the story is when I was invited to go out to eat with the Nitwits—I kind of made it happen. There is this all you can eat place that just opened up and I wanted to go; I wanted to go anywhere away from our kitchen. Mom decided to get out a cookbook and try something new. I think she likes color more than tastes and no matter what is put on my plate or how much, I have to eat it. Dad says it's rude if I don't eat all Mom cooks. Well at least it's what's *cooked*. (You know next time, anything raw, I am not eating—raw isn't cooked. I'll use that one, but Dad will most likely say: "Fine, but eat all the cooked parts." Those are the ones I don't want to eat. Oh, well, I better save that one for when Mom serves some raw pigeon, which for fancy people is called squab, or some other *fancy* food; yeah, that's when I'll use that one!) I don't know that she'll serve raw pigeon, but she gets a little wild once in awhile and makes something real crazy. One time it was this exotic food that we had to eat with our hands. It's weird to touch little bits of unknown meat with your fingers. I guess I eat burgers and fries and pizzas and cookies and apples and bananas with my hands but unidentifiable wet squishy meat? Another time dinner was cooked in a huge pumpkin, not a state fair live inside like James and his peach pumpkin, but bigger than the Thanksgiving turkey pumpkin. Mom can make it weird.

This day Mom was going the weird route. Don't get me wrong, sometimes Mom cooks some interesting things and, although she uses a cookbook, I think the problem is that she doesn't really follow the recipes all that closely. This time, it may have been the super-pink bologna that she bought at the deli earlier in the day that set my plan in action.

I was with her all day shopping. I hate those days. They are so boring and she won't let me bring a game and she won't let me hang out at the TV store and she won't let me get an ice cream or anything. When I was younger, I would hang out under those circular clothes displays. Mom would have to get security to find me because most of the time I would fall asleep or sometimes some lady would scream when she was poking around the new summer dresses and find me, and I would have to hang out with the security guard until they found Mom or one of my sisters. My sisters would be so mad, because their faces would be half-shaded in free thick orangey makeup and they would look more ghoulish than normal. I'm too big for those clothes racks now, but I would even hang out now in the bookstore and read books, probably all comic books, but Mom says that is stealing if I read more than a page or two, but then why do they put all the tables and chairs and benches everywhere? They want you to read.

So Mom had bought the pink meat and then two purple eggplants. I generally like eggplant, but Mom bought some deep green mint jelly and some black berries, pinkish-orange salmon and little green Brussels sprouts and this almost black bread . . . black bread . . . isn't that just burnt toast? Oh, and then some very red Vietnamese hot sauce. She even bought some edible orange flowers. I did not want to be home.

Since I seemed to be getting involved with so much stuff with the Nitwits, I sort of invited myself over to their house and hung out until dinnertime. I was helping Grandpa Nitwit take out all the batteries from the flash lights and smoke detectors and radios . . . because he told me he heard on the TV that you want to make sure your batteries were fresh in an emergency.

"Won't be useful if we use up all their power just sitting in them things," Grandpa Nitwit said. He put all the batteries in a veggie-bag and put them in the refrigerator crisper. "Want to keep them as fresh as possible," he said.

Well, I used the 'if I didn't accept their offer it would be rude' rule and Mom had to let me go with the Nitwits to dinner. I didn't pick up on what I should have picked up on about their dinner plans. I wished I had. I don't know what I would have done differently, but I should have seen it coming. You can give a guess now if you like, but I'll tell you a little more. We were in their minivan and everything was normal, everything was going well, and believe it or not we went to Ruth-Anne's All-You-Can-Eat Country Fixin's. I sort of promoted it by telling Dad Nitwit that it was all you can eat. He sort of perked up at that. This is when I should have seen it coming.

"Yes," I said, "and it is real home cooking and it's all you can eat."

"All you can eat?" Dad Nitwit smiled. "I've never been to one of those places. I wonder how they stay in business. Where does everyone sit?"

"At tables," I said. I didn't get what he was getting to. I should have seen it coming.

"All you can eat," Dad Nitwit repeated.

"Yep, economical," I said.

So we drove to RuthAnne's All-You-Can-Eat Country Fixin's. I loaded up on chicken fried steak and some tri-tip and cheesy potatoes. I know you get to go back and get more, but why bother getting up when you can just pile it high.

I should have known something was up. The Nitwits didn't get much on their plates. In fact, on the ride over, they seemed really curious, too curious about the whole all you can eat concept. Dad Nitwit asked me at least five times: "All you can eat? Really? All of it?"

"Yes," I said every time. "It is RuthAnne's All-You-Can-Eat Country Fixin's, and that means all you can eat."

"Wow. It sure is an opportunity to eat some interesting things. The restaurant is all you can eat."

"That is the point," I said. "You eat things that you don't normally do, or you can eat a ton of what you love, but never get at home."

"Hmmm, I see," said Dad Nitwit.

I led the way and I piled my plate high and, tonight, I was glad not to be eating Mom's cooking . . . but what the Nitwits did . . . I guess I was glad to be there too or I never would have believed it. Even though it was the Nitwits, I don't think I would have believed it without seeing it. Go ahead and guess now. I bet like one in a thousand of you can guess. Okay, here it is—

Uh, Mom's looking for me right now. My sister Aggie was in an accident. She's okay. See, a car hit her friend's car at a stop light at like one mile an hour. It will take one of those magic paint pens to fix the bumper. It was probably just noise; they probably didn't even feel anything, but Aggie has been on the phones all afternoon telling and texting her friends how Olivia and she were almost killed. I even heard her say: "Olivia almost killed us!" Way to treat a friend!

Well Mom is making me bring Aggie all her food or whatever, basically anything she wants: DVD's, CD's, magazines, brushes, whatever. It's not like she will even watch or listen to anything with that phone implanted in her ear. This is so way beyond texting. It's like any other day, but more annoying.

Mom says that Aggie is fragile at this time. My goodness, another time, a couple of years ago, when we went camping in the mountains, Aggie wouldn't come out of the tent because she had a zit and she didn't want to be seen— by WHOM?!!! Smokey the Bear doesn't care!!! His cousins might, and she did put all this banana or coconut or melon scented cream all over her face, but no big black bear tore through the tent and licked her face clean. When that happened to the other girl years ago, it must have been awesome. The girl was alright. I don't know if I told you that. Her husband, guess what, ran right out of the tent. He said he was going to get some pots and pans.

Bear kisses, now that is what I wish I could make happen with my sisters. That would be epic.

Well, on this camping trip there were two or three other families around us. They all had kids or grandparents, so I had to be her little butler, her look out, her basic servant for two days. Mom said she understood Aggie and Aggie was fragile at this time and blah blah blah. If Mom says she understands, then that is the law. I wish she would understand me more often. I do so much for my sisters and they do nothing!

The truth was there was a boy from our local high school there, Dylan. That's what it was. Why didn't she just pop the little red puss-filled carbuncle and move on. No, I had to go to the village store instead of fishing or swimming and get those creams and stuff. I bought the smelliest one I could find, but no bear tore through the tent. When I did get back, my sister Trudy said she needed a new pink razor and some girly deodorant. I thought this was camping and rough-ing it . . . and they're the ones that like to shop. Why did I have to do this?! I had to get all that stuff and magazines with boys all over the covers, things like Tiger Beat—Tiger Beat? Really? What kind of title is that? They didn't have any Marvel comics at the store, only DC, but whatever. Bat-man, The Flash, and Green Lantern are cool, but Weather Wizard—come on! Why name him Weather Wizard. Do a simple combination like the Pokemon names; something like The Wizther would be so much better.

So here was my sister up in her room going all dramatic over a half a mile an hour car-kiss, and I became her servant once again.

Oh, while we were camping on the second night, I invited Dylan over for s'mores. I made sure Aggie had just put on her cream (I guess pimples are more dangerous than bears) when I asked Dylan to help me get the stuff from the tent. He saw her in all her spotted white face glory. It was great, but two days later she kept pinching me on the ride home. I think I still have a scar.

Mom made Aggie some soup. It had nothing to do with color combinations, it was just straight forward chicken noodle soup. However, Mom always puts something extra in it, like a hundred tabs of vitamin C. They don't quite disintegrate and the taste is horrible. Gramps chews them constantly. I do not know how he does it.

The Nitwits didn't take any soup at RuthAnne's All-You-Can-Eat Country Fixin's, and they certainly weren't going for the stuff with vitamin C. They went through the line and all, and got some food, but they seemed disinterested.

I jumped right into my meal. It was sloppy. I went for my napkin, but it was gone, not totally gone. Want to guess? Want to guess what happened? I should have seen it coming. Here it is. It was in Big Sis Nitwit's mouth, yeah, not around her mouth, in it—she was eating it. Then the tablecloth tugged and my drink fell over. Sure enough, Aunt Nitwit was chewing on the table cloth like a goat. I saw Lil' Bro

Nitwit going at the breadbasket, not at the bread, but the basket.

"Whoa," I said. "What is going on here?"

"Well," Dad Nitwit said, "it's All-You-Can-Eat, so we thought we would find out all the things we *can* eat."

"Huh?" I said.

"This is great," said Grandpa Nitwit. He was biting his chair. "Doesn't fill you up, but it sure is fun." He kept chewing at the brown vinyl.

They kept eating if that is what you can call it. I shook my head and said between bites of real food, "This isn't the witch's house in Hansel and Gretel. This isn't Willy Wonka's place." They didn't get what I was saying.

I shook my head some more, but it didn't feel good with a ton a food in my mouth, so I finished my barbecue and went to get the peach cobbler, the apple pie, the berries and cream, some western ravioli with extra meat sauce, a crumbly-chocolate pudding with extra shaved chocolate on top, another soda—you know, all the good stuff you are supposed to get at an all-you-can-eat joint.

The Nitwits, well, let me tell you about the Nitwits. I tried to explain to the manager that I was not a part of their family and that I shouldn't be banned, but I think he saw how much I ate or how much I didn't. Hey, but I did take a bite of just about everything . . . that was food! The Nitwits kept eating everything else. They didn't eat the metal flatware or the plastic cups, but they ate or took a bite of just about everything else. They nibbled on cushions, wall hangings, wood molding, specialty menus, other tables' tablecloths, those fake flowers in the middle of the table, just about everything. It was amazing, and you know what, I'm the one, yeah, I'm the one that when we were back on Hartland St. had the stomach ache. Go figure!

They were finally kicked out of the restaurant after about a half an hour of trying all they *can* eat. Amazing, I know.

What is amazing is that I haven't been interrupted in the last twenty minutes. My sisters are up to something. They are probably planning something with my parents to make me do more of their chores. I think I will sneak downstairs and see what is going on. I'm a little hungry. Some grapes or maybe some trail mix sounds good. Yeah, a bag of trail mix will sit just right . . . the nuts, chocolates, and raisins, not the bag!

So if you are ever asked, "Why were the Nitwits kicked out of an All-You-Can-Eat restaurant?"

They tried; they tried to eat it all: the food, the napkins, the straws, the tablecloths, the breadbaskets, the drapes, the waiter's shirt. . . .

10

SOMETHING'S FISHY

I have another one to tell you about my neighbors, but first my sister Trudy, oh, has she done it. She was dating this one boy, Harvest, yeah his name is Harvest, everyone calls him Harvey, but I called him Harvest for the first couple of weeks. I told Trudy to watch out, if he wants you to look at *the* Harvest moon—haha. Mom made me stop saying it and made me keep my pants up while I was around her and him. Dad for some reason called him Rabbit Boy and Mom called him Pooka or something like that, but only when Trudy and Harvest weren't around. Well, I think Trudy was getting sick of it so she started dating another boy. His name is Richard, but the best part is—go ahead and guess. The best part is she didn't tell Rabbit Poo; I combined my parents' Rabbit and Pooka names. Trudy so hates that: Rabbit Poo.

So Trudy didn't tell Rabbit Poo and here is the real best part. Go ahead and guess this one. I bet some of you get it right away. Here it is; it's so great—Trudy got caught—today. Both Rabbit Poo and Richard showed up to the house. Okay, this wasn't even the greatest thing. What Trudy did to herself was the greatest thing. Oh, it is so great; it's epic. Want to guess on this one too? I don't think any of you have a chance and getting it. I'll tell you I don't even care that I had to help clean up downstairs, the stairs, and the hallway, even though she should be the one cleaning up everything! It is so great.

Okay, where Richard lives allows him to cut through the woods, so he showed up at the back door. Rabbit *the Harvester of* Poo was at the front door. Mom, when she figured out what was happening was going to make Trudy talk to both of them at the same time, but POOF! no one could find Trudy. At first it was funny to watch Trudy running from front to back to back to front, but then she disappeared. No one could find her until we heard her on the side yard screaming at the top of her lungs.

She was trying to get away. She knew they were going to see or hear each other soon, so she climbed out on the second story roof over Grandma's long room and slipped down to the ground. She slipped again and again too. She didn't plan ahead. She was in the dog run and well, we have been watching the Liuzzi's three Labs, three one hundred and twenty pound Labs. We watch them all the time; the Liuzzis go on a ton of vacations.

Yeah, Trudy didn't think ahead and, when she slipped to the ground, she landed, let me say in a Lab accident, definitely a *large* experiment gone wrong. You know, Labs, especially these Labs, eat a lot; I mean a lot. I don't think there was a square inch in that dog run that hadn't experienced a Lab accident. They were like three crazy Santa Clauses—they left presents everywhere . . . and Trudy seemed to be unwrapping them all. I am talking full-on no hand-breaking face plants. She slipped, screamed, fell, faced-planted, rose, tried to get to the door, and did it all again. It was awesome. I sneaked some pix on my ancient phone, but Mom took it away from me before I could upload it. I've got to get it back—it is epic, but Mom probably erased it.

It was so great when I arrived outside. The first thing I saw was one of her many, and I mean many, face-plants. It was so great even though I knew what was coming. She was going to get out and race to her room, and I knew that I would have to clean it all. Mom would totally make me do it because Trudy would have been humiliated in front of the boys and need time to recover . . . I have heard it before! So I grabbed the hose and I put it on jet and let it fly. Mom let me keep it up. She figured out what would happen too. I doused Trudy; I was very helpful. I kept her right in front of me and it was full on jet stream. Trudy still made a mess in the house, but I blasted so much water and made so many puddles, she kept slipping.

Richard and Rabbit *the Harvest Moon* Poo just gawked at it all. They seemed to be smiling and laughing. They figured it out, why Trudy was there in the dog run. I guess they also figured out that she got what she deserved. Mom sent them home. They went toward the woods looking at their cell phones talking and laughing. I've never seen her move so fast. Want to guess. Go ahead and guess who moved like a cheetah on fire and then like a four-handed pickpocket. Let me break this one down:

My parents are very aware of the Internet and how things never ever leave the Internet, so when my mom saw the boys looking at their phones and just knew they had taken some video of Trudy doing her doodie-ballet, she did not want her daughter out on the World Wide Web in such a state. Mom thought of one thing and only one thing and that was to get rid of that video. She took off so fast and tackled Rabbit Pooh, a good form tackle too, right around his waist. She smashed him to the ground and ripped his phone out of his hand. She bounced up and Richard just tossed his phone to her. Mom has gotten really savvy with all the apps on all the devices and she deleted the videos before Rabbit Pooh even stood up. She surely checked the phones and the social apps, smiled at them, and gave the phones back, and definitely said while patting them on the back and directing them quickly to the woods, 'You are such sweet boys; have a nice day.' I wish I had a video of that. That would be so awesome. I think Mom would even appreciate how good of a tackle she made.

I was done in the house and picking up the wet mess in the dog run when there went the Nitwits with a fish tank in a wagon. You know, they seemed to do this every week. I'd seen this before; curiosity was killing me.

I didn't know why they took their fish tank to the aquarium store every week, but they're Nitwits and I was curious, so I kind of spread every thing around the side yard and hustled over the street. I had noticed that there did seem to be different amounts and different kinds of fish in the tank almost every time I looked. There were always those orange fish, yeah, you guessed it, goldfish, sometimes some black striped fish, and whatever freshwater fish there was, but mostly goldfish. I have a cousin, in another state, who loves Goldfish crackers. He eats them with everything. He puts them on pizza, in his dinner salad his mom makes him have every night, and on fish when he goes backpacking, fish on fish. He loves them so much, he gives them up for Lent. He gives them up for six weeks. He really does like them. I should give the Nitwits a box of Goldfish crackers and see what they do with them.

So the Nitwits, well Big Bro Nitwit and Big Sis Nitwit, were taking their fish tank back to the aquarium store. I didn't need or want anything at the fish store, but it had to be good; I had to follow them. The Nitwits you know sure make things interesting, but this seemed normal, almost too normal; then I saw Brent, my cousin . . . hahaha.

Brent was at the coffee shop near the aquarium store. He had on a crazy green French hat and was talking into a microphone. Guess what he was doing. Go ahead and guess. I'm sure some of you know what he was doing, but I bet none of you knows what he was using. Well, here it is: He was reading poetry. Yeah, he was reading poetry into a microphone and wearing a crazy green beret, but I'm sure there is something none of you knows. He wasn't reading his own poetry and he wasn't reading that old stuff every crazed English teacher makes every student read where no one knows what's being said or understands even half the words that are written. No, he was reading from a kid's poetry book called *Chickens Don't Have Fingers*, and he was doing it with some drums (they call them bongos), and he was making all these faces and hootin' and hollerin'. It was a crack-up. I was laughing. No one else was.

Big Bro Nitwit and Big Sis Nitwit went into the fish store on their own. I stayed and watched my cousin, who I think should go to another state. A cousin like this should be the one who is from somewhere else. I guess he is from some-where else—Renovo, PA, but he lives with us now! All the people sipping coffee were either texting, reading, or just kind of staring into space; well, okay a few were listening with wide open eyes and drumming fingers. Those were the ones with the super-jumbo-grande-cups in front of them.

I have to share how it was. You can guess but it had to be seen. This is how his poetry recital went:

Bongo Bongo Bongo—that's the sound that was being made, on the bongo.

Bongo Bongo Bongo Bongobongobongobongbongbobobobo.

"Skadattle," Brent said with a little punch.

Bongo Bongo Bongo.

"Skadittle." *Bon Bon Bon Bongo.*

"I'm big." *Bongo.*

"I'm little." Bongo.

Screeching: "I'm anything I want to be." *Bon Bon Bon Bongo Bongo Bongo Bongo Bongo Bon Bon Bongo Bongo Bongo.*

Brent stood up and pointed out toward the crowd, the four people watching him.

"And you." *Bon Bon Bon Bon Bon.* "Should judge." *Bongo Bongo.* He was now yelling as loud as he could. "My size."

He paused for about five seconds.

"By the actions." *BonBonBonBonBonBonBonBonBonBon-BonBonBonBonBon.*

"I devise." Bongo.

"What I do." Brent got real soft for a moment . . . *bongo . . . bongo . . . bongo . . . bonGO.*

"TruLY! . . . defines . . . me." . . . . *Bongo.*

Oh, all the faces he was making and all the arms he was throwing and all the spit he was spraying—it was golden; it was hilarious; it, well part of it, was caught on my older-than-the-hills cell phone ('For emergencies only,' Mom said when she gave it back to me absent all but one of Trudy's pix . . . which is epic) that could hold like twenty seconds of video.

It's twenty seconds of gold though. Brent's face is all twisted and he spat all over the place. He was so passionate. It was kid's poetry but he was into it. What is great and this is so great, and I didn't see it at the time but I caught it on my sisters' hand-me-down phone, he spat into some dude's coffee. Yeah, a big white glob went hurling into this dude's coffee and then the dude went and drank it like almost immediately. Maybe he should have been watching Brent instead of staring at his computer screen. It was when Brent said 'but'. Haha, it's a 'but spit'. I can say 'but spit'—it's grammar. Beep and Eddie are going to love that one. Beep will be all 'beep 'but spit' . . . classic.' Brent's 'but spit' went flying like twenty feet. It is epic and Brent so will not want this on the Internet. That dude would probably hunt him down and I don't know what coffee dudes do, probably just give him something to ponder—haha.

Well, the coffee drinkers simply drank, except for the four, or more like ten, who were now paying attention to him. They clapped this weird little dainty old lady clap. Brent took it like it was a standing ovation after a grand slam in the World Series. He was happy. So was I; this was great. I just knew that the next time he went in my room and punched me or stole something this was going on You-Tube.

Back to the Nitwits, Big Bro Nitwit and Big Sis Nitwit were done. Big Sis Nitwit had a new big pooper-scooper. Why they sold that at the fish shop, I had no idea. I asked why she had bought it. She said she liked big bowls of ice cream. She said that, "It says *Super-Scooper*, so the scoop must be super and then I will have a super ice-cream scoop." I didn't like the mental picture that put in my head. Remind me not to have dessert over at their house. I am shaking my head right now . . . Nitwits!!!

So it didn't seem to be anything *ordinary* for the Nitwits. Then we got to their house. Right away Big Sis Nitwit tried her Super-Scooper *ice-cream* scoop. She tried to get it into a half-gallon of chocolate-chip mint, but no luck.

I said, "looks like it scoops up the whole carton."

Big Sis Nitwit smiled. She scooped up the carton with her Super-Scooper, took out a serving spoon, those big ones for salads and pastas and stuff, and started to eat. She smiled at me again and again while on her way to eating the whole thing . . . but not the carton . . . she tore that open and licked it clean, but she didn't eat it.

Mom Nitwit came into the family room. "Oh look at the fish."

"Bought some new ones today," said Big Bro Nitwit.

"Good, they don't seem to last," Mom Nitwit said with a smile.

"Why not?" I asked.

"I guess Nature can be real cruel," said Mom Nitwit. She put her face closer to the tank and wiggled. "But I do like them. Oooh-oooh-hooo."

Mom Nitwit paused a moment and then waved at the fish. "Hi there little fishy fishy fishy fish." She tapped on the tank, which everyone knows you are not supposed to do.

91

"You're not supposed to do that. It's like a sonic boom," I said.

"Sonic booms are cool," said Lil' Bro Nitwit.

I shook my head. "You've got me there," I said. Sonic booms are cool, unless they are Gramps'—you know what I mean. You know, he rules sonic booms.

Well, maybe the fish like sonic booms. Anyone ever ask a fish?

Mom Nitwit just smiled really wide and stared at them with wide eyes. "Did you feed them?" she asked Big Bro Nitwit.

"Not yet," said Big Bro Nitwit, as if it were the most obvious thing in the world.

"You have to feed the fish?" I asked. I didn't think any of the Nitwits had any chores; remember the whole garbage can thing. Well, just then the cat came in. I didn't think they had a cat either. Well, Big Bro Nitwit put his hand in the fish tank, grabbed a fish, and squirted it between his fingers and palm and shot it toward the cat.

"There," he told his mom.

"Oh, what did you do?" Mom Nitwit looked startled.

"I fed the fish," said Big Bro Nitwit.

"Oh," she said still semi-surprised. "Is that what the man at the fish store says you do?"

Big Bro Nitwit shrugged his shoulders. "I fed the fish."

"Okay," said Mom Nitwit. She left.

I was dumfounded. "That's how you feed the fish, huh?"

Big Bro Nitwit looked at me as if I asked if the sky were blue.

It was time for dinner so I left. Grandma was making eggplant tacos—they're good.

When Brent got home, he went straight to my room. He still had his bongo drums under his arm. He took my phone. He deleted my video cache. It's okay. I had already sent the file to Beep and Eddie. It was on a flash drive in a couple of seconds. I knew I'd get it back and get Brent back too and I knew I could use it when I needed to. That's it. I'm going to use it to get him to help me finally get this kiss done. He didn't even check the video when he deleted it. He has no idea about the 'but spit'. I'm going to show it to him and get him going. This is so much better than a monkey-scrub.

I'm going to get more eggplant tacos. Today has made me hungry, so I'll just get right to it. If you're ever asked, "Why is the Nitwit's fish tank always empty at the end of the week?"

Big Bro Nitwit was told to feed the fish . . . and he did . . . to the cat!

11

GROWTH SPURT

Okay, so I'm outside all the time. I have all the chores as you may have noticed. I know, not all the chores, but all the outside chores and any project that comes up that is outside and that even counts things that are inside but somehow find the energy within my sisters to come outside. If it is outside it screams Joe, and so I spend a lot of time outside. I like the outside. So much more goes on outside that is interesting than inside, even though I mean outside our house and outside and inside other people's houses.

Well, this is right outside of our house. Grandma decided she wanted what she called a victory garden. When I was nine, some woman named Heather told me that in Britain they planted spinach because it was perpetual. She was really impressed that I knew what perpetual meant, so she kept talking to us. I was writing a report on spinach and Mom bought me a shirt that said *Delicious Spinach*. That is what started the conversation with Heather. She saw my spinach shirt and started talking. "I hope you like spinach," she said. She was old. She was in World War II. She wasn't a soldier; she was a kid. She said they had spinach all the time because it grew all the time in their, guess what, in their victory gardens. This was so perfect for my report on spinach. My teacher even said how great it was that my report contained quotes from real live people. Yeah, Heather's sister, her older sister, Maureen, came over. First thing she said, want to guess, you got it, she said, "I hope you like spinach." They both said it in this old English lady accent. Then their even older brother came over. Yeah, he said 'I hope you like spinach' as well. His accent was really *Wallace and Gromit* thick. I tried to speak like them for weeks. I must have said as thickly as I could, "I'm Trevor, hope you like spinach." I'd follow it up with a squeaky Heather and a helium Maureen. I must have said 'I hope you like spinach' 20,000 times until Trudy threw a tantrum about how annoying I was and she couldn't study—yeah right, more like she couldn't IM. Oh, and I do like spinach.

Well, it's kind of nice to plant some, well, plants, and see them grow, and I tell you the little tomatoes right off the vine, hot from the sun, are like candy, candy fruit, yum. All you moms and grandmas that want your kids and grandkids to eat healthier, plant those little tomatoes; they are awesome. You kids, you should try them—they're great. You have to get them right off the vine when they are hot and then a little rub on your jeans and a pop into your mouth—great.

So I had to build a fence around the garden, put in posts, hang a gate, bury the chicken wire eight inches deep—Dad helped . . . even Brent helped. I think something about rent was mentioned to Brent. Gramps sat and watched and laughed and laughed and laughed and he didn't have any beans. Not yet, he had a bunch of seed bags—for beans! We didn't know it at the time, but they grew when all was said and done and Mom cooked them, and well, you know. I'm sure that wasn't the only reason he laughed. Sometimes he just sits there and laughs. That's Gramps.

We were near finished with the fence and Grandma brought out all this stuff she bought online, bags and bags of stuff, none of it for planting. The first thing I had to do was rub some sort of oil over the posts. It stunk and I had no idea what it was for. The second thing I had to do was hang all these little brown sacks around the fence. There must have been forty of these little brown sacks. Grandma told me to pat them to get the aroma out. I did it; I had no idea what they were, and I did it everyday for weeks. That's forty sacks a day, 280 times a week, over 1,000 times a month I patted the little suckers. I bet you have no idea what was in them. I had no idea. I'd tell you to guess, but I doubt one of you would even be close. You could guess.

Here it is: They were bags of coyote pee!!! I bet you had no idea—I didn't. I was squeezing bags of coyote pee with my bare hands day after day for weeks, over 1,000 times. It's unbelievable. Grandma bought pee. Who buys pee?!!! It's bad enough that manure is bovine poo, but who buys bags of pee . . . coyote pee?!!! Grandma actually bought pee . . . uhhhhh!

Here is the breakdown: Grandma bought bags of coyote pee because some magazine said they were good for keeping out squirrels. So to keep out the squirrels, I had coyote pee all over my hands, not the liquid pee but the pee dust. Liquid stuff I might have been able to identify right away and wash it off, but flakes, I had no idea, and they got on my clothes, under my fingernails, in my hair, up my nose. How many nights did I go to bed with coyote pee flakes all over and even *in* me?!!! Grandma!!!

I had coyote pee dust all over me for weeks and weeks when I finally found out what was in the bags. You know who knew? I bet you do. This one I totally bet you know who did. I went right upstairs . . . to my sisters' beds. They knew and didn't tell me anything. I rubbed my hands all over those sheets like a cat rubbing itself in a vat of catnip. I climbed in their beds like Goldilock's brother and wiggled all over. I put a pee-bag each in between their mattresses and box-springs. I would have even remade their beds if they ever made them in them first place. I don't know if the pee-bags do anything, but it is the thought that cheers me up. I better check between my mattress and box-spring. . . . Okay, nothing there but a dead cricket.

Grandma asked Dad if he would electrify the fence. Gramps laughed. Yeah, Gramps just laughed. I just knew he had designs on the victory garden.

I'm whispering now. I don't think Gramps likes Grandma!!! I know the exclamation points don't mean whispering, but I'm telling you a secret of sorts and it is really explosive information.

Well, we had planted some squash, some watermelon, some zucchini, some spinach, some tomatoes, some basil, some cilantro, some Greek oregano, some English thyme, some lemon sage, some green and purple string beans (not the kind that Gramps likes, but he did secretly plant his seeds), some eggplant, a whole bunch of stuff. It was going well, until—

Oh no, Gramps is grumbling *loudly* for me. He must have heard me writing about him. Oh well, see, I cleaned his bathroom today. It is DISGUSTING! He has a certain type of problem and he has to use this tube thing when he makes . . . ah . . . number one. It's called a catheter.

Well, I think that he mis-aims on purpose. He has too. Every time I'm near that bathroom and he is going, he just laughs and laughs and then wouldn't you know it, his laundry basket is full, full of towels I have had to use to clean up the mess he has made. At least I don't have to do that laundry . . . yet. What *do* my sisters do? Sisters . . . uhhhhh. I swear I have to do more than coyote pee bags in their beds. I've got to do something big, something real big, something crazy, way crazy . . . like . . . like the kiss. I have to make them kiss Big Bro Nitwit! There, I've told you part of my plan. That is why I've been telling you about the Nitwits. Big Bro Nitwit is the kisser. I still have to tell him. Ahhhhhhh! He just has to be, and the kiss has to be done and it has to be now. Ahhhhhhh!

Okay, so one of them has to kiss Big Bro Nitwit. I've been delayed too much, but I need help. I'm going to force Brent. I am going to confront him with the videos of himself, the bongos and the skater crash and more. Tonight I'll make him commit to me to getting my sisters or at least one of them. I don't think I'd ever be able to get all three of them. So one it will be. Simple, a kiss, a Nitwit, and a video: It will be awesomely epic.

Okay, I have a bunch to do but Brent isn't here so let me finish this one. My sister Trudy is the oldest, and she mistakenly mentioned something about wanting to be a nurse, so mom makes her deal with Gramps' and Grandma's laundry. I'm not sure how that is connected but hey, it lets me have a break. Trudy wants to deliver babies; babies do poop all over themselves and it does get all over the place, so it is good practice, especially with Gramps and Grandma.

I still don't know why I have to clean his bathroom. Don't nurses need to work in a sterile environment? Trudy should do this too. I'd suggest it, but some argument will be brought up that if I collected the towels shouldn't I launder them. I'm keeping my mouth shut for now. For one reason, and this is gross, but Gramps doesn't always use the toilet paper when he is in the toilet. Yeah, sometimes he uses the towels. I don't know why, but I will find the tub full of towels with the goop he uses with his—condition—and that have a whole bunch of something else!!! I go in there and I hear him in the next room. He just laughs and laughs. . . .

I didn't do anything much differently today, so I don't know what the problem can be. I better go check out why Gramps is yelling now.

It was nothing. I went there and Gramps started laughing. I left him there giggling to himself watching baseball. I like it when baseball season is in full steam. Gramps watches everything, every game: pros, college, Little League, Japanese, whatever he can find. He's nuts about baseball. Once in awhile we have a catch. That's nice and he's taught me how to twist the bat to get extra punch on the ball, but he doesn't go to any games anymore not after he—

Oh no! Now it is Grandma; she's yelling for me. I better check this out. If I don't respond to these two, I really get it—from, uhhhhh, my sisters. That is simply another reason why one of them has to kiss Big Bro Nitwit. It's killing me. It's brilliant. I have to do it!!! My sisters lay it on me like

I kick puppies or drown kittens if I don't help G 'n' G—immediately! Sisters . . . double uhhhhh!!!

I know it is because they don't want to help G 'n' G. But seriously, my sisters go off on Gramps and Grandma as if they were a three headed mom, but they don't get scolded and given chores, yet they say things about G 'n' G like "They're old'; "They need your help"; "They are your grand-parents"; "They smell"; "They are so annoying"; "Grandma's intolerable." That was Cece. She let it slip once and Mom heard. Hehehehe, Cece was in so much hot water.

Let me break it down: See one time, Grandma went through all of Cece's letters and her diary and all she did the next few days was make the sign of the cross in front of Cece. It drove Cece crazy, which made me happy as a dog with ten tails—that happy. Cece didn't know why it was hap-pening (none of us did) until she reread a page in her dairy that Grandma had written on. Cece came down stairs yell-ing about privacy and individuality, but Mom said Grandma probably thought it was one of those memoir books everyone writes these days. Cece didn't believe it, but she's moved the diary around a few times. Right now it's in her underwear drawer. Yeah, I know where it is. I need ammunition in this house and don't worry, I use gloves and tongs; I do.

I better go see what is happening.

So I had to help Grandma. I had to go into her bath-room. It, in truth, is worse than Gramps'. It's normally disgusting. She has her blue-flecked toothpaste stuck to the basin and all her different yellow and beige and white creams in globs on the counter and on the floor not to mention her wet patches that she tosses everywhere and then there is the stuff I actually touched near her bed. It turned out this time that she wanted to take her weekly shower. See, most of the time she gets her hair done and then just puts different perfumes all over herself for the rest of the week. One whiff, one gentle breeze, one wave of a folding paper fan ten feet away from her and her air will knock you over. I mean it—that bad! There shouldn't be a law about trashcans; there should be a law about smelly grandparents.

Wouldn't you know, Gramps had been in Grandma's bathroom. Want to know how I knew. Let me just say that all her towels were in her tub, and she doesn't get that dirty. Even though she stinks and leaves sticky globs and hairy pads, she doesn't get *that* dirty. Mom made me tidy up the whole place. It took close to an hour. I better not get this as another chore. Yes, I had to touch her . . . her girly stuff again!!! Uhhhhhhhhhh!!!

Oh, back to the victory garden, it was a victory. I still don't know why it is called a victory garden unless you feel victorious for growing something, but grilled squash and eggplant with crispy cheese are great, and those tomatoes yum . . . and when the watermelon is chilled, woohoo. Here, here to farmers. Food right from the ground is great!

Yeah, it was going well until we had a break-in. It wasn't from an animal or a thief; it was from a Nitwit—Lil' Bro Nitwit. Boy, did he tear up the place one morning. He took out all of our pumpkins and some of our beans (the ones that Gramps doesn't like). He must have dug up a dozen plants and replaced them with little mounds. We at first had no idea.

We found out it was he later in the day. He came right over with a pitcher of water and some Miracle-Gro. Gramps was at the window laughing, so Dad peeked outside to see why Gramps was laughing this time. Dad held me back. I was angry with Lil' Bro Nitwit, but Dad wanted to see what Lil' Bro Nitwit was doing. He wanted to get Lil' Bro Nitwit's action over his words. I think he figured Lil' Bro Nitwit might not explain himself well. So Dad and I watched as Gramps laughed.

All Lil' Bro Nitwit did was mix the Miracle-Gro in the water and pour it over the mounds he had created. As he did this, we saw a whole bunch of colors exposed as the dirt washed away from the tops of the mounds.

Dad finally let us go outside. He didn't yell or anything. He simply asked Lil' Bro Nitwit if he needed help. I guess Dad figured the damage was done, let the kid finish his experiment.

I was still angry and I told Lil' Bro Nitwit those things weren't going to grow and they were plastic or rubber to boot. He shrugged. I pulled one out of the ground. It was a rubber 'p'. It was from a baby's matt—the ones that have cutout letters of the entire alphabet for little kids to crawl all over and learn the letter shapes. I bent and grabbed another one, a plastic refrigerator letter.

"What is this?" I asked. "Trying to make vegetable soup?" I laughed. I thought it was funny. Dad gave me one of those dad-disapproving looks, like *I* had been tearing up the garden all morning. Ugh!

"Joe is right Lil' Bro Nitwit. This is a garden for growing vegetables and fruits, not plastic toys."

I picked up more letters. They were all p's and u's stuck next to each other. I didn't get what he was doing, but Lil' Bro Nitwit grabbed them out of my hands and shoved them back into the ground.

Dad stooped down and picked out a pair of letters and spoke sternly. "Lil' Bro Nitwit this is Grandma's victory garden; this is not your garden. What you did here is wrong."

I nodded and smiled. This was something. Dad was disciplining someone else. I wondered if I could give Lil' Bro Nitwit one of my chores.

"Now please explain yourself," said Dad.

I don't think any of you guys can get this one. You can try and guess, but I don't think you'll get it. Now, don't read on and then say, oh yeah, that was my guess. Go ahead and guess and see if you are even close. You may want to go back and look at all the facts—there is a good challenge: Go back and look at the facts and then guess what Lil' Bro Nitwit was doing. Go ahead.

Did you go back and think about it. Well, if you did or didn't, here it is. It turns out that Lil' Bro Nitwit had a plan. As Dad was backing him up into a corner and picking up all the letters, Lil' Bro Nitwit said that he buried the u's and p's and brought over the Miracle Gro, because he was tired of being Lil'.

Lil' Bro Nitwit said, "Mr. Christmas, I put in a bunch of u's and p's together in your garden and watered them with Miracle Gro so I can grow up fast. I'm tired of being Lil' Bro Nitwit. I figure it is about time I'm simply a Nitwit."

That is what he said.

Well, now you know, and if you are ever asked: "Why did Lil' Bro Nitwit bury u's and p's in the garden and douse them with Miracle Gro?"

He wanted to grow *up*, grow *up* fast. Kids these days! They want to grow up so fast.

Oh, Dad left a couple of small mounds with u's and p's in the garden. Dads do this I guess. I even let Lil' Bro Nitwit pour Miracle-Gro on them . . . after he helped weeding. That was a good move by Dad.

The thing is that Lil' Bro Nitwit hasn't grown an inch and he has stopped coming over to pour his Miracle-Gro and I am left alone to weed Grandma's victory garden. Uhhhhh, where are my sisters? They eat!

12

Say Cheese

This is something you should know: The Nitwits have a baby goat. They stole it. They didn't mean to, but they did. I was with them, not when it was actually stolen, but I was there at the place.

See, I went out to eat with them again—yeah. Mom went shopping. The restaurant was another buffet type place, this time at a farm. The restaurant is right there on the farm. The sweet corn is unbelievable. This is the way to get kids to eat vegetables, moms and grandmas—sweet corn, fresh sweet corn right off the grill. It doesn't even need the bucket of butter that's on the table at these farm restaurants. The kids will eat it. The Nitwit story is right in there— getting the *kids* to eat. Go ahead and guess right now if you want.

At dinner everything went all right. No one ate my napkin or the breadbasket or anything like that. It was eerie how normal it was, but I have found that sometimes everything falls into place and normalcy creeps into the Nitwits lives, but, of course, it was temporary. See, when we went back to the car, a goat was in the backseat. Dad Nitwit just shrugged his shoulders knowingly, got into the car and, but for three shirt collars being sampled and a hat being eaten, the drive home was just fine and now . . . the Nitwits have a goat.

The goat was in the car because—

Oh brother, my sister Aggie is yelling for me. I'm not going. I'm going to hang out on the roof. I know it is off limits but then she won't look there for me. I bet it is a G or G thing, and of course, Aggie just wants to sit on the phone for the next five hours. I'm outta here.

So the goat was in the car because Grandma Nitwit said it would be good cheese and it would keep the lawn cut.

Lil' Bro Nitwit asked if all goats were made out of cheese. Grandma Nitwit said, "I don't think so, but when goats get older they make cheese."

Big Sis Nitwit asked, "Do they wear those funny little nets on their heads when they make cheese, like the people who make cheese do?"

Mom Nitwit said, "Of course they don't; those people are in a factory, a goat is in a barn."

"So they wear straw hats," said Big Bro Nitwit.

"That's right son," said Dad Nitwit.

I shook my head and mumbled, "You *must* be *kid*ding me."

I'll tell you, now, the one thing is if you get close to their goat, you are going to get your pants chewed off. I know, I know for a fact, that the Nitwits actually play a 'get your pants eaten' game. I don't know if this was part of the game, but Lil' Bro Nitwit was just standing there one day and making faces at the goat and wouldn't you know it his shorts came right off and the goat was going to town chewing away on Lil' Bro Nitwit's shorts. (The goat must think it is the Nitwits' All-You-Can-Eat family restaurant.) Lil' Bro Nitwit seemed to be okay with it, standing there in his tighty whities, laughing. Yeah, the Nitwits definitely play the 'get your pants eaten' game.

So let me go back. This is what happened at the farm, and no one stopped Dad Nitwit. He simply went and did it—right out in the open, in broad daylight. He went to the farm part of the farm restaurant and unlocked a gate, walked over to a young goat, put a rope around her neck, led it over to his car and put it in. That is what he did. You know, I bet some of you can figure out why he did it. Go ahead give a guess.

Okay whether you guessed or not, here it is; the sign in the front of the farm restaurant read:

"With every paying adult . . . one kid is free."

Yep, that is what it read. I know, poorly written sign. It should have read: 'Kids eat for free.' The farm was lucky. I figure the Nitwits only took one kid because Dad Nitwit was the only *paying* adult.

They still have the goat. It is like the cat: It seems to show up whenever. Oh, I have to get going. Beep and I are going to go TP'ing our friend Alex's house tonight and we have to get all our supplies together. I know I am delaying the kiss, but TP'ing a house is great fun.

So if you are ever asked: "Why did the Nitwits leave the farm restaurant with a goat?"

The sign read: "With every paying adult . . . one kid is free," so Dad Nitwit paid and took one.

13

WaSN'T eVeN HiS BiRTHDaY

Today reminds me of a day not too long ago. I'll get back to today in a second, but first, it was a really humid day. Going outside in my regular clothes felt like jumping in a pool in my regular clothes. You know I spend most of my time outside. I probably was outside because all three of my sisters were inside, and Grandma and Gramps were inside, and if I'm out of earshot of Mom, I don't have to clean up after anybody's mess, so I was outside. Man, it was so humid and not even breakfast time. I was dripping pretty well when Big Bro Nitwit and Dad Nitwit and Grandpa Nitwit had a stand-up pool delivered . . . only delivered, so yep, they planned to put it up themselves. I know—crazy.

It looked right, the structure and everything. The Nitwits actually put it up rather quickly and soundly. The Nitwits can

111

sure stick to their tasks, but man, it took forever to fill it up. They invited me over to go in, but there was barely any water in it.

This is what they were doing. They had read that it took 13,000 gallons to fill up the pool, so they thought they were real economical by not buying 13,000 individual gallons of water but by using an old milk jug, gallon size, and filling it up with the hose and dumping it into the pool. Yep, they were going to do this 13,000 times. At least they didn't fill it up with 13,000 actual gallon jugs!

So Big Bro Nitwit said, as he went from the hose and carried the gallon of water over to the pool, "See, Joe," he tapped his head and then lifted the leaky gallon jug, "we didn't have to buy all those gallons of water. We got one right here." He was as proud as a cat presenting two dead mice.

I rolled my eyes. "This is going to take forever."

"But think of all the money we are saving," said Dad Nitwit, a big smile across his face. He looked like he had three dead mice for show and tell.

I stood back and watched for about ten minutes before I could take it no longer. This was going to take weeks, not to mention all the water being wasted by Big Bro Nitwit not bothering to turn off the hose while he walked to the pool, and who knew why he didn't fill it up with the hose right at the pool. Oh, we all know—Nitwits.

I grabbed the hose, walked over to the pool, and flung it over the side. I said, "This way when you are not filling up the gallon, the extra is going right into the pool. You won't waste any—"

"How will we know how many gallons go in?" Grandpa Nitwit said, a look of disgust glaring at me. He flung the hose out.

"You'll know when it is full," I said.

He simply stared at me and shook his head. I was a little creeped out.

Awful, awful—I have to cook one meal a week now. Total sneak attack—Mom just sneaked right up on me and told me that I have to assist in the kitchen once a week by cooking a dinner. Apparently my sister, Aggie, complained this afternoon to Mom that I don't help around the house. Are you kidding me!!! Around the house, that's what I do, everything around the house!!! That's it! She is so going to kiss Big Bro Nitwit. She's the one.

She's the one! I wasn't sure. Aggie is the one! They all drive me crazy, but this is the last straw. I mean it. She's kissing Big Bro Nitwit and it's happening ASAP. Brent better be home at a decent time tonight or I'm getting the flash drive and pressing send and his 'but spit' will be all over the internet and that dude at the coffee shop is going to hunt him down and *bongo* him. We have to come up with something good. I can't just have Big Bro Nitwit walk up to her and kiss her. That would cause all sorts of trouble. I have to get Aggie to do it herself . . . but how!

Unbelievable, I do everything around the outside of the house and bathrooms and crazy messes. Are you kidding me? You know why this happened. I bet you can guess why. Here is the breakdown. My sisters are awful cooks, awful. That's why; they know it too. My sisters know they are awful and they want me to cook because I actually care what people are going to eat. I actually will pay attention to the directions and follow them! I actually like cooking, but making me cook, that is a whole other thing. Mom says I start tonight! Ridiculous! Mom has some meeting or something to go to this evening and thought it would be nice if I cooked tonight. All my sisters have their precious activities, so I have to go cook. I didn't take out anything to prepare so I have to scramble. Pasta! I'll make pasta, but I can't keep it that simple. I'll have to make it with chicken or sausage or something. Brent better show up!

Okay, dinner last night—yeah it was last night, another night without the kiss. I know; it's driving me crazy too. I'm totally shaking my head. Aggie is so getting it!

So dinner last night, I'll tell you the truth, it was weird, but it was good. I cooked chicken simple in a pan, and I wanted a sauce and I thought it was good to put a little heat in it so I added some chili powder. I liked it; Gramps liked it. He laughed a bunch. Grandma ate; Mom and Dad ate; my sisters hated it. My sisters wouldn't even touch it. See, I wanted to have a sauce with a kick. I don't know how to make a sauce, so I used the only sauce I could find and it was from a famous company and it is used around the world and most everybody loves it. It was from Pennsylvania. It was thick and rich and, well, brown and you probably guessed it. Go ahead and guess. I bet a bunch of you guys can figure it out. Well, here it is—it was Hershey's chocolate sauce. Yeah, I used Hershey's chocolate sauce on pan-seared chicken.

Hey, I found out that in Mexican restaurants, chocolate sauce on chicken, they have it; you can order it; it's called, mole, but it is pronounced moh-ley. If you know any Nitwits, don't let them read this part. They will go home and serve chicken with a hairy little blind critter or a single-haired black bumpy face-skin glob on it. Remember it is pronounced moh-ley, so don't go around telling everybody in the waiting area at Rosie's Cantina that they have home made *moles* on the chicken.

Oh well, I chopped a salad and heated some bread and cut the cheese . . . the mozzarella cheese! My sisters, though, they forgot one thing. They didn't compliment me. They complained. Their cooking nights are coming up. You know, I don't know if this is a good thing. I don't have to cook again this week, but you know, I liked it. I'd cook again. I'd even cook what I made last night, a little less chili powder, but chocolate with chicken—yeah-yeah. You know, and don't tell my sisters this, but I'd cook a couple of nights a week. It would eliminate some of Mom's color coded concoctions and my sisters' messes. In fact, just to learn something new, and to annoy my sisters, I will cook once a week. Oh, and even though I'm having fun with it, I'm still so mad at Aggie. It shouldn't be a chore; it should be something I ask to do, something I want to do to help out.

You know, next time I cook, I'll plan it out. Mom and Grandma have a ton of books. I know how to bake Grandma's cookies. I should bake something like lasagna or something—oh, lasagna with chocolate sauce, a chocolate lasagna—yeah. I think my sisters are going to love it!!! There is a cheese they use in cannolis, those crispy Italian folded cookies, so why not chocolate in lasagna? Probably not, but maybe something that looks like chocolate.

So dinner last night was okay. Brent came home after I was asleep, so no movement on the kiss. I'd wake him up in the morning, but he'd sleeper-hold me and I have to watch out for the spit flying all over the place. I don't know if the videos are worth that.

Well, back to the pool. I went home, drank a ton of milk, put a hole in the carton, one a little bigger than a hose nozzle, and brought it over to the Nitwits' backyard.

I said, "Here is another gallon, but watch this." I went over to the pool and put the hose in the carton. "As it fills up the gallon, it fills up the pool." I nodded my head quickly.

They went for it. I don't know why. I think they lost count of the gallons they had put in—all twenty-two of them or something. It was going well, but it was taking forever. All the kids who heard about the delivery and watched the construction had pretty much left.

Lil' Bro Nitwit was the one really getting itchy. He really wanted to swim in his new pool, so he took the other gallon, put a hole in it and grabbed the Canfield's (the Nitwits' neighbors) hose and *borrowed* some of their water. Two hoses really make a difference. Then he went inside and tried to drink a gallon of punch, which he couldn't, so he poured the extra, which was most of the punch, into the fish tank, put a hole in the jug, and brought over the Canfield's front hose. Three hoses really make a difference . . . to Mr. Canfield's water bill. You know, my dad always says to buy the longer hose, the longer extension cord, the longer computer wire, because you will always need that extra foot or two to finish a job. I wonder what Mr. Canfield would say.

Toward the end of the day, word got around that the pool was filling up faster and almost every kid in the neighborhood, even kids with pools, were trickling back . . . with swimsuits under their shorts . . . waiting, waiting to be invited to swim.

Finally, the pool wasn't filled, but it had enough water in it for actual swimming and Mom Nitwit was okay with all the neighborhood kids going in in their shorts, (she couldn't see how bulky they were with suits underneath them) but she told Big Bro Nitwit, Big Sis Nitwit, and Lil' Bro Nitwit and even Grandpa Nitwit that they each had to get their suits.

"Suits for all of you or you can't go swimming," said Mom Nitwit.

"Which one?" asked Big Sis Nitwit.

"Whichever one you have," said Mom Nitwit. So the Nitwit kids and Grandpa Nitwit went rushing into the house to get their suits.

The pool was fun. Some friends of mine have the aboveground pools and some have in-ground pools. We have an in-ground pool, but the Nitwits' pool was new, so it was more fun. There must have been twenty kids in the pool in the first two seconds Mom Nitwit said it was okay to go in. Some of those who wore shorts over their swimsuits were so excited they didn't even take off their shorts.

We were all in before the Nitwits had changed into their suits. Big Bro Nitwit came out and Big Sis Nitwit came out and they made some big splashes. Grandpa Nitwit made an even bigger one and his snorkel and mask went flying off, but Lil' Bro Nitwit was nowhere to be seen.

When he was seen, well, only a few people actually saw him, but it was enough to clear the pool. It certainly was. You want to guess why? Do you? Go ahead and guess. It is unbelievable even for a Nitwit . . . okay, maybe not for a Nitwit. Here it is:

Mom Nitwit had said suits for all her children and Grandpa Nitwit. I told you that. "Suits for all of you or you can't go swimming." That is what she said.

Well, like I said, Big Bro Nitwit and Big Sis Nitwit changed pretty quickly and joined everyone. Lil' Bro Nitwit, though he took a little while, came flying out of the house. Want to guess right now. Okay, he ran as fast as he could by Mom Nitwit, scooted up the ladder and splashed into the water, but some of us saw, yep some saw—he was . . . he was like a jaybird as people say. He was like his Grandma on the way to the post office except without the stamps—at least she had stamps! Yep, Lil' Bro Nitwit burst out of the house and sprinted past his mom and jumped in the pool naked, naked in front of God and all.

He splashed about and finally came up from the depths of the four and a half feet of water as everyone scrambled to the side and some jumped out, girls screaming, boys screaming.

"What . . . the . . . beep?" cried Beep as he went over the side.

Water was everywhere. The screaming rose as Mr. Canfield joined in, screaming about his hoses. I think one had a leak at the faucet, so his back porch wasn't looking too good.

Mom Nitwit finally ambled to the edge of the pool and asked, "Lil' Bro Nitwit why are you swimming in the pool naked?"

"A pool is where you are supposed to swim," said Lil' Bro Nitwit.

"Yes," she said.

119

I thought she was going to leave it at that, but she repeated, "Why are you naked? Where is your suit?"

"I have it," Lil' Bro Nitwit said.

"Where?"

"It's all over me."

"What is all over you?"

"My suit," said Lil' Bro Nitwit.

"Un-beep-believable," said Beep from the huddled mass of kids.

Mom Nitwit simply stared, bewildered.

Lil' Bro Nitwit offered, "It was the only suit I could find."

"What do you mean it was the only suit you can find?" said Mom Nitwit. "You are not wearing a suit."

"Yes I am," said Lil' Bro Nitwit. "I'm wearing my first one."

"Your first one? You can't fit in your first one."

"Yes, I can."

"How?" asked Mom Nitwit.

"It's exactly my size," said Lil' Bro Nitwit.

Mom Nitwit scrunched her brow. She was confused.

Lil' Bro Nitwit must have sensed it, so he offered, "I'm wearing a suit; I'm wearing my birthday suit."

"Beep."

"Oh," said Mom Nitwit a bit of understanding coming to her face.

"It was the only one I could find," repeated Lil' Bro Nit-wit.

"Oh . . . birthday suit . . . birthday suit . . . I guess that counts." Mom Nitwit gave a little smile and turned to the house.

"Beep, beep, beep, beep, beep."

Yeah, I totally agreed with Beep. He and I didn't go back in the pool that day . . . no one else went back in the pool that day . . . except the Nitwits. I think going in the pool right now would be great. I'm going to go swim . . . with my suit on, my navy blue surf trunks that is.

So if you are ever asked, "Why did Lil' Bro Nitwit jump in his pool naked?"

He could only find his *birthday* suit . . . and his mom was okay with that.

14

THE 'LAST' POP-TART

I've broken plenty of things—I'm a boy. I've broken plates, glasses, windows, fences, and of course plenty of wind! Oh, this reminds me of a story; it's pretty funny. A few years ago, at one of Trudy's plays, I had plenty of wind to break. I had eaten all the baked beans we had left over from some barbecue or something; Mom wanted me to. You all know I was given a mission to keep them away from Gramps and Mom didn't want them wasted and so they were my breakfast with eggs, lunch with chicken cutlets, and my afternoon snack all by themselves. Gramps wasn't going with us to the show. Well, let me just say that after the intermission there were no people sitting in the row in front of us and no people sitting in the row behind us. Beep was there, toward the front. When I told him later what happened, I was his hero. He was all 'What the beep?'; 'That is beep awesome'. He was also glad he didn't see me earlier and beg his mom to sit with me.

Mom said, "I wonder what could have happened to everyone; the show is wonderful." Dad shook his head. Aggie and Cece tried to sit with friends and even *frenemies*, but Mom wouldn't let them. I think one of the boys in front of us was in Cece's class. He turned around a few times with such a sour face. I just smiled. My sisters hid behind their collars that they pulled up in front of their faces. Cece kept misting a little perfume bottle and Aggie had the cleanest hands in the world—she went through an entire little bottle of some almond scented antibacterial gel.

Mom kept saying, "I don't know what the problem is." Cece and Aggie were about to protest when Dad said, "He's got a case of the *arse*." (That is one of Gramps' favorite sayings. Anytime someone else lets one go he says, 'He's got a case of the *arse*.' He never says it about himself though.) "That's what the problem is," said Dad. "He's got a case of the *arse*."

I tried to say something, but Mom stepped in and made everybody go back to our row. We were all alone. It was kind of weird and let me tell you, I didn't stop. I was Old Faithful but with much less time between explosions. Let me tell you—I stunk! When the play was over, my sisters were out of the auditorium in seconds. Mom let them go home with other people and just kept saying, 'Wasn't that a pleasant time?' Dad rolled his eyes and shook his head—he wanted me out of there but Mom wanted all of us to support Trudy. I don't think this is the support she would have wanted.

"I think that was lovely," Mom said. She was really pouring it on. She knew what had happened, but was not giving in. Moms cover for their sons once in awhile—especially when they are the ones who make me eat three bowls of beans before we go to a play and I get a case of the you know what.

When we got home and Gramps 'got wind' of what happened, he laughed and laughed and laughed. He gave me a hi-five like I was a champion or something. My sisters gave me evil stares for a week. That was a boy from Cece's class in front of us. I think he brought it up with her a few times— hahaha. I bet he thinks she was doing some of it, like it was a family ailment.

So I've broken plenty of things; I've even broken some bones, but I've never broken someone else's bone and certainly not on purpose. Yeah, I'm talking about a Nitwit now. I'm talking about Big Sis Nitwit. Big Sis Nitwit did it, broke someone's bone, and she did it on purpose. She used a lamp. She did it right in front of her mom, and Big Sis Nitwit didn't even get in trouble. Can you believe it! Crazy, I know . . . and on purpose . . . right in front of her mom. Nitwits!

There was some sort of argument going on. I just had one: Who would win, Rogue of the X-Men or Batman?

Would Rogue suck the life out of Batman before he could get one of his gadgets free to chemically change Rogue or something? Batman is still a regular man of course, and for me, an X-Men girl could whip him in a second.

This wasn't the argument the Nitwits were having. This is the one that I just had with Brent until he grabbed me and gave me a monkey-scrub. He couldn't win the argument so he went to the violence. Twice I told him if I were Rogue and he were Batman he would be dead already. I was going to tell him a third time when he said, "So you want to be a girl?"

That was like what a tick does! So tick!

I still fought, but I knew what was next and I escaped before it became a loogie-noogie—those wet monkey-scrubs are sick and he's really good at them. Man, those bongo pictures are hitting the Internet. Hold on, maybe I can set the file up on Beep's account and get a code word, a total spy-movie thing, and tell Brent about it and if Beep doesn't here from me or he gets the code word, he pushes the button of no-return and Brent's 'but spit' is in that dude's coffee and everyone can see! He can call up one of his poet buddies to ask Aggie on a date and at the right time somehow switch to Big Bro Nitwit and yeah, a big sloppy kiss and a big sloppy picture. This will be great. That won't work—ahhhhhhhhhh. I've got to think of something better.

Well, the argument the Nitwits were having and it was between two Nitwits, was who ate the last Pop-Tart. Now, it was Big Sis Nitwit. I was there. She had half of the skinny strawberry treat (I prefer blueberry) in her hand and crumbs on her face and shirt. She ate it . . . but she kept saying, "I haven't eaten the last Pop-Tart. I haven't eaten the last Pop-Tart."

This all reminds me of my sixth grade math teacher, Mr. Tomato, that is what we call him, his name was Tomachko, who kept telling us that "The good die young or the good die young." All he did was repeat the same words over and over and over and over while shouting some of the words so it sounded like: "The GOOD die young or the good DIE young or THE good die YOUNG or THE GOOD DIE young or THE GOOD DIE YOUNG." He certainly got excited about things and sixth graders can get excited about things too; the problem was that no one knew what the *hectare* he was excited about. It was math class and he kept telling us that the good die—hardly pleasant—and what in the name of Pi it had to do with math, I have no idea.

Well, it turns out that all Mr. Tomato was trying to do or to say was that good people either die at a young age like twenty or something or good people die with a young happy attitude toward life. I guess, like Gramps, he laughs a lot and seems to go about his day with his own thoughts and actions and gets along with everyone and still gets surprised about things, that when he dies, he will be THE GOOD die YOUNG!!! Just kidding. People will say that he was one with the good attitude. He is a good guy, a little crazy, but normal crazy, but a good guy.

Mom's friend Dezri died young both ways. She just turned forty. That may seem old to some of you, but it's not. She died young. She was such a happy person, always traveling with her kids. Yeah, she was young. Mom cried a lot. It was cancer.

Cancer is so tick . . . so Major Tick!

Back to The Good Die Young—the only thing I don't like about this saying is that the opposite would mean that rotten people die old. Well, some old people do seem rotten if not only smell rotten, sort of like my Grandmother with all of her perfumes and her hairspray, or they do rotten things once in awhile like my Aunt Jess using my shoulder as a hankie. So tick!

Well, Mr. Tomato didn't make it sound that clear whereas Big Sis Nitwit kept eating the last Pop-Tart during her argument and wasn't that clear on the account of eating the whole time. All Big Sis Nitwit was trying to say was that technically the last Pop-Tart wasn't gone, but she just kept saying: "I haven't eaten the last Pop-Tart. I haven't eaten the last Pop-Tart. I haven't eaten the last Pop-Tart."

Let me break it down: It had a bit of the same logic Mr. Tomato was using—like repetition is going to clear things up. Big Sis Nitwit didn't eat the last Pop-Tart because some was still in her hand, so the last one was the one before the one she was eating. She wasn't done; therefore it hadn't

128

been eaten. I guess she was making this argument, but, well, she was eating the last Pop-Tart. It was obvious. Of course, *she* didn't think so . . . she's a Nitwit.

Big Sis Nitwit said again, with a tenth of her Pop-Tart left, "I haven't eaten the last Pop-Tart."

Big Bro Nitwit finally said, "Gimme a break."

I bet you can guess this one. How it exactly happened, maybe not, but I'm sure most of you know what happened next. I've pretty much told you already. Here it is: Big Sis Nitwit hit her brother with a lamp, one of those heavy gold-plated things that have that moving arm so you can move the light to read. She hit Big Bro Nitwit right on the left arm. Mom Nitwit witnessed the whole thing. Mom Nitwit didn't scream or anything at Big Sis Nitwit. I couldn't believe it. I was speechless.

"Come here," she said to Big Bro Nitwit.

"Okay," he said. He didn't even cry or yell or anything. The look on his face was like what had happened was a normal thing. Maybe it was for them, but for me it was absolutely crazy.

"It's broken alright."

"Yep," he said.

"You asked for it," Mom Nitwit said in a completely normal tone.

"Yep," Big Bro Nitwit said.

Mom Nitwit looked at me standing there with my mouth wide open and my eyes as big as bicycle wheels and said, "What can I do? Big Bro Nitwit said, 'gimme me a break.'"

I thought Big Sis Nitwit looked ready to take another swing. The Nitwits get focused. It looked like she was struggling to keep the lamp back as if the lamp had intentions of its own.

"I did say it," said Big Bro Nitwit.

"Yes, he did say it."

"What did he say?" asked Grandma Nitwit who came into the room.

"Gimme a break," said Lil' Bro Nitwit.

Yeah, you can guess again. Big Sis Nitwit took a swing. She was focused. Lil' Bro Nitwit was in no mood to be broken and jumped out of the way . . . right toward me. I scrambled out of my seat to get away from Big Sis Nitwit. I knocked into the table supporting the fish tank; water shifted and a wave came pouring over the edge; a few fish went flopping. The cat appeared like a ghost through a wall and had a meal.

"Ahhhh, uh, ahhhh," was all I could say. I couldn't even say stop or anything. Luckily Mom Nitwit grabbed Big Bro Nitwit, took him outside, and summoned the ambulance, the one that hangs on the street all the time, on account of the Nitwits.

Big Sis Nitwit stared at me. This must be the feeling a Zebra has who catches sight of a lion staring at it from the tall grass, the really close tall grass. Finally my brain started working and I asked if she finished the last Pop-Tart yet.

"I haven't had the last Pop-Tart," she said.

She darted her head around like a chicken until she found the last bit on the carpet. She picked it up, smiled at me, and popped it her mouth. I could see that it was wet from the fish tank splash. She didn't seem to care. I went home a little faster than usual, totally happy I didn't get involved in the Pop-Tart argument.

I wonder if we have any Pop-Tarts. Probably not, but Grandma may have made something. I'm going to go check.

Well, if you are ever asked: "Why did Big Sis Nitwit break Big Bro Nitwit's arm with a lamp?"

He said in an argument over a Pop-Tart, "Gimme me a break." She did.

15

No Cat's Meow

Someone broke into some houses on our street. Aggie is calling everyone and telling them a homicidal maniac is on the loose, only on our street of course. (I say homicidal psycho jungle cat; I like Calvin and Hobbes—go check out that book). Aggie milks everything. I swear, a little cut on her and she has gangrene or she twists her ankle and here comes Gramps' electric scooter that he never uses, and then all her friends come over and bring her DVD's and cupcakes, okay, some of the cupcakes are good, and magazines, the magazines are lame. I told you about that zit earlier.

Ugh, Aubrey Reynolds—she's like the Grandma's old lady friends that always squeeze my face. Thankfully, she didn't show up, none of the girls did—it was all the boys who showed up.

I don't think Brent cares for a lot of the boys that like Aggie. There is something there for me to think about.

Well, the stupid cat burglar has really made it bad around here, but no one has, or should I say had seen him, except, you guessed it, a Nitwit.

You can ask right now: Why did Big Bro Nitwit not call the police when he saw his neighbor's house being ransacked by a cat burglar?

You can guess now if you want, but I'll break it down for you. Here is what happened:

See, Big Bro Nitwit was feeling sick yesterday morning. He stayed home from school. He went outside—

Oh brother, we have this class project for a fundraiser and Mom is in charge, so of course, I have to help her with everything. It's something I can't even get—it's a skateboard. Dad doesn't want me to have a skateboard. 'Too many injuries,' he says. Of course football is fine, but I'm cool with that—football is fun.

Oh, one time when he was around fourteen, Brent broke a few ribs skateboarding—probably Dad's reason against skateboards. The video's somewhere. Dad might have it, for evidence of his anti-skating stance. I think I mentioned it before but didn't give you the details. I so want to see it again. He was trying to slide down a rail, you know, those metal handrails next to concrete stairs. He didn't make it and bang, he landed on the rail, with his chest and his lower region—if you know what I mean. It was totally tick for him. I need to find that video. It's both great and awful. His body flings around like a cartoon character. You can hear the crack, not really, but it is that vivid. I bet Brent hears it and *feels* it every time he sees it: Bang—Crack—Ow . . . TICK!

I don't think you could guess this one in a million years. You can give it a try. Big Bro Nitwit was "feeling" sick, so what did he do. Any ideas? Okay, I'll tell you this: He claimed he had boils. Any ideas? Remember, he is a Nitwit. So have you given it some thought? I doubt you have it right. Here it is. Big Bro Nitwit sat in an ice-pool trying to cool down his boils—yeah, Nitwits!

Does Big Bro Nitwit have some boils or at least had some boils? Who knows really, probably a few spider bites or something. Really, boils? That's Bible and plague stuff. I like the word carbuncle, myself. It hides the idea of giant red puss-filled growths on your neck and back that when bumped ooze (great word, you should use it as much as possible, especially around sisters) yellow phlegmy (another great sister word – phlegm) gunk down your shirt or pants. If you get those phlegmy carbuncles (superior combination), they are always on your back, in an area where you can never really scratch them. I'm just saying. It just seems that that is where they go. Okay I had one, not a boil but a carbuncle, and it was on my leg. I could scratch it, but most go where you can't get to them without some sort of crazy wire hanger thingy you bend into fifty angles.

Speaking about itching like crazy, I had a cast and I swear a flea went down it and was biting the living bejeezies out of me for the first week I had it. Mom would not let me stick anything down there. She read a hair-dryer would help, but of course my sisters, when my sisters heard this, hid all of theirs. Wouldn't want to help out their brother. Sisters . . . uhhhhh!

Well, I was so sick of it, the carbuncle on my leg, so I jabbed it with a fork. It popped and it oozed—all that yellow phlegmy gunk and some blood of course. I should have done it at dinner or something, right in front of Trudy, Cece, and Aggie. Gramps would have laughed, but I did it by myself. I showed Beep and Eddie. Beep of course said it was beep fantastic; Eddie said that it looked like it hurt. It *was* beep fantastic, but it *did* hurt, a bunch, but it was cool. . . . It really hurt.

When Gramps saw it, he said it would make a good mark and a good story. Gramps has so many marks on him and there are multiple stories about them all. I didn't show Mom what I did until my carbuncle reformed and grew even bigger and darker and really smelly brownish goo started coming out of it and it hurt, really hurt, way more than before—totally tick. I had used the fork I used at lunch. I don't think I cleaned it. The carbuncle was pounding and pounding and then the brown turned to red and yellow and . . . it wasn't good. I had to go to the doctor and he lanced it or something, but the scar is cool. Oh, and even though I was in a lot of pain, another good thing is that I kept sneaking up on my sisters and showing them my bubbling carbuncle before it hurt too much. One time, Aggie was sleeping on the couch. I pulled a chair right up to her. I nudged her. It was great. The scream, I can still hear it.

So Big Bro Nitwit had boils and of course boils are hot so he made himself an ice-water bath in a kiddie pool, not the big pool—he didn't have enough ice—and sat in it all day long. (I don't think he got up to do anything—yeah, anything. You know what I mean. He had brought a large pitcher of lemonade or something with him, so you know what I mean.) He was there and of course this is when the cat burglar that had been reported in our neighborhood went in and out of the Canfield's house taking a TV and a computer and a guitar and a few boxes of stuff and a—

Oh brother, the project, I gotta go.

Dad. Dad! DAD! Dad wanted to make sure that the skateboard worked properly, so even though I am not allowed to own one or even ride one, it had to be tested. He tested it. I bet you can figure out what happened when my dad tested the skateboard. Go ahead and guess this one. Yeah, Dad went and tested it and Mom took him to the ambulance at the end of the street. It's a good thing it is there. We've used it a lot lately. Well, a few times, well once, never actually—no one has ridden in it. We've gone to use it a couple of times but there is always a Nitwit getting attention or being transported to St. Brigid's.

Aggie put her fist through the front door window a few months ago. I was in the house and the door was locked, which is odd, because someone is always home. Aunt Jess or Gramps or Grandma is always here. Well, I pretended that I didn't hear her at the door, and of course she didn't have a key, and I sauntered toward the kitchen and she blew a gasket, so she put her hand through the window. Is getting in the house that important? There are probably five open windows and the door in back can be jimmied open in a second. Sisters . . . uhhhhh! Oh, and who knocks on the glass. You knock on wood—that is how the saying goes. It is quite obvious that knocking on glass is not lucky.

I grudgingly walked Aggie to the ambulance, but Big Sis Nitwit was getting bandaged, so was Grandma Nitwit. Big Sis was happy to see Aggie, like it was some reunion or something. Well, Aggie went right to her phone and called all her friends and as she was getting some spray on her knuckles she reported to all that she almost "amputated her hand, major arteries were involved, severing." Yeah, it was all that. Then there was the "He's so gorgeous." He is Darren, one of the paramedics. All the pain talk went away and it was all little giggles, which is pretty good, because even though she didn't need stitches, she bloodied herself up pretty good. The bandages were cool, but she wouldn't let me peek under them to see her wounds. Sisters . . . uhhhhh!

Mom is taking Dad to Dr. Feingold right now for a more in-depth diagnosis. Dad hurt his wrist and shoulder pretty good. This is great. No, not that Dad is hurt, but they will be gone and there are a bunch of boys around, all concerned about the cat burglar of course, and Brent should be home early, so the kiss! The kiss can happen tonight! Right now! Big Bro Nitwit still has boils (so he claims). Oh, this is perfect. It's going to be perfect. Maybe Big Bro Nitwit has one on his face near his lips—oh, too good!

Well, real quick, while I am thinking of it, the Canfield's came home and called the police. Officer Hawkins and some rookie, Officer Grohl, came; they saw Big Bro Nitwit and of course asked him why he didn't get up and call the police station or even shout to anyone nearby when he saw the cat burglar. Guess what Big Bro Nitwit said, go ahead, guess. Did you get this one? Some of you guys probably have a good idea. This is what happened:

Officer Grohl was new and looked like he needed a pot of coffee. He was not familiar with the Nitwits yet, but you could see him shaking. Yeah, he probably needed a fresh pot of coffee. Officer Hawkins went on with Big Bro Nitwit. "Did you see him take a TV?" asked Officer Hawkins.

"Yes," said Big Bro Nitwit.

"Did you see him take a computer?"

"Yes."

"A guitar?"

"Yes," said Big Bro Nitwit.

139

Officer Hawkins was perplexed; Officer Grohl was steaming. He looked like he wanted to strangle Big Bro Nitwit. He couldn't believe what he was hearing.

"Some boxes? Did you see him take some boxes?" said Officer Hawkins.

"Yes," said Big Bro Nitwit like he had said yes to all the other questions.

Officer Grohl finally screeched: "So why didn't you tell anyone? Why didn't you get up and call the police? Why didn't you tell anyone about the cat burglar? You saw all of this and didn't call the police. Haven't you heard about the cat burglar?"

"Yes," said Big Bro Nitwit.

Officer Grohl steamed even more. "Then why didn't you call the police if you heard about him!"

Big Bro Nitwit stared into the face of Officer Grohl and simply said—do you know; did you guess it—he said, "He didn't have a cat."

Officer Grohl was frozen for a second then shouted, "We know that!"

Big Bro Nitwit looked a bit confused. "Then what is the problem?"

"Cat burglars don't take cats!" shouted Officer Grohl. I think he was getting boils.

Big Bro Nitwit stood there in silence, scratching his back with a tree branch. Officer Hawkins motioned to Officer Grohl and the rookie stormed off mumbling to himself. Nitwits can do that to you.

Officer Hawkins looked at Big Bro Nitwit, and looked around the neighborhood and looked at the Nitwits' house. Everything looked normal. That's how the Nitwits are, sometimes everything looks normal. Officer Hawkins wrote something down, took another look around and at Big Bro Nitwit, who had plopped back into his kiddie pool, shook his head, shrugged, and left.

So if you are ever asked: "Why didn't Big Bro Nitwit call the police when he saw his neighbor's house being ransacked by a cat burglar?"

The burglar didn't take a cat.

Okay, quickly, this is were we stand. I think you know enough about the Nitwits to understand why it is going to be perfect to have Aggie kiss Big Bro Nitwit. It is all going to work now. Mom and Dad are gone; Aggie is home; Brent just came home; Big Bro Nitwit is Big Bro Nitwit.

It's going to be perfect. I'm outta here.

16

PUCKER UP

Okay, so it is going to happen in about ten minutes. It's going to be perfect.

Let me break down what is going to happen. This is what we have going on: Mom and Dad are at Dr. Feingold's. I sneaked into Dad's office and found some CD's. I found one marked 'skateboard'—pay dirt. I showed the videos of Brent to Brent, and Eddie and Beep have the code words if he doesn't follow through although it sounds like they are on their way over here. Gramps was given a spicy bean burrito. I made a big, oh-my scene, and the tents are up. Aggie is out there with all her boyfriends pawing over her. Grandma is still in the house and Aunt Jess is somewhere. It might rain. It couldn't be more perfect.

Brent and I came up with the perfect idea. Brent takes a film course so he needs to make films. He is behind schedule so he has to do something, something quick. So he approached Aggie and her beaus with the idea of doing a 'see who gets the date' game. He told them a game show was the format he needed to film. They all went for it. The dudes even helped us set up the stage. We are right in front of Gramps' shed. We have a divider tarp and chairs and we put a hole with a little flap in the tarp for the secret kiss.

I painted a big sign in red: Kiss and Tell. That is what Brent is calling the show. It is your basic couples show. The girl asks some questions—the guys answer. We, however, are putting in the blind kiss to make it more interesting. Aggie will have to kiss the boys and tell which one was the best kisser. This is so gross it is great. That is when Big Bro Nitwit is going to sneak in and kiss Aggie. I'm going to offer ten bucks to one of the guys to step aside. No, wait, I'll just tell Brent to bring in bonus contestant number four just for the kiss. Oh, it's going to be perfect.

Rabbit Poo just showed up. He heard people were here and he wanted to tell them in person. It's pretty cool news. It's cool he came by to tell it. He and his dad caught the cat burglar. The rat was in their garage. Rabbit Poo said they opened the garage door and there he was. The door to the house had locked and when the thief went for it, Rabbit Poo bounded into the garage and tackled him. He said the burglar was small, like 120 pounds or something. He said that his dad sat on him until the police arrived. Wow, Rabbit Poo is a real hero. Everyone is so stoked for him—a real hero. I think Trudy mentioned something about going out with him again—sisters . . . uhhhhh!

Here we go, and we better be quick. It's definitely going to rain.

Okay, here is a quick write; I want to give it to you fresh.

Things are a little behind schedule. We are in the shed. The rain came quick and hard. Brent is still going for it, but it is cramped in here. I hope we can get some good video. We have too. We don't have much time. Mom and Dad are probably going to be home soon and I bet Mom wouldn't want Aggie to be in a kissing video. Mom has that thing about the Internet. Aggie kissing Big Bro Nitwit—it's going to be perfect! Gotta go. . . .

It wasn't perfect. It could have been perfect. It could have been better than perfect. We could have gotten some good video, but . . . I can't believe it. I can't even write about it yet. Unbelievable, that is all I can say right now. Unbelievable. I bet, no I know, you cannot even guess what happened.

We went into the shed because of the rain. I had stuffed Big Bro Nitwit there earlier and he was still hiding in his spot. We had the chairs set and the tarp hanging but Brent needed more lighting. He went to get some lamps from inside the house. That is when things started to go wrong—really wrong.

When we began to move stuff to find a place to put the lamps, Robbie, *mimbo* number two (Brent says that good looking dumb jock dudes are called mimbos) found the electric train with which Gramps and Dad and I used to fiddle. He turned it on. He didn't notice that the roof had a leak and it was right above the battery. He turned it on while he rested his hand on the metal tracks. He didn't really fly or explode, but he did get a whooping shock that moved him backwards rather quickly right into another puddle that caught his foot and sent him head back and head first into a toolbox. He was lights out. I wasn't filming at the time. Brent had the recorder. That would have been great.

Andrew (mimbo number one) got a little scared and fell over a chair and knocked the tarp onto Aggie who started screaming like a banshee. Andrew got up to help her, but he tripped over Robbie and went smashing into one of Gramps' sea sponge bins (ones that are shallow and open aired) head first, and of course he grabbed onto it as water splashed from it and he slipped still holding onto the bin that fell right over onto him as he fell to the floor, where he bumped his head and was knocked out. Mimbo three, Eddie, he jumped up on a shelf to get away from the water but the shelf was not a strong shelf and when it started to creak, he grabbed higher only to grab hold of Beep's dead cat which freaked him out so much that he jumped from the shelf right over a trashcan, a robot trashcan, and as he went head over heals and landed on the other side of the trashcan, the trashcan went head over heals and disgorged its contents, which for some reason I never removed after Big Bro Nitwit's dance exhibition, right on and all over the now knocked out Eddie. Brent and I still weren't rolling video.

Gramps opened the door. He was giggling. Aggie just kept yelling. Brent came in with Rabbit Poo. Hail was coming down the size of ping-pong balls. The noise was tremendous . . . from Aggie. The dogs were loose—chasing the Nitwits' goat. The goat scampered into the shed and the dogs bolted in after and ran all over the mimbos getting sticky brown glop all over their bodies and faces. The dogs left the goat alone and attacked the doll heads and flung them all about; then they got the cat—boy did they have fun with that. Gramps let one fly and then another. Now you want to guess what happened next. I bet you don't even know what happened. It is unbelievable. It is everything I wanted and didn't want. Did you guess? Well, here it is.

Big Bro Nitwit came out of hiding. He had all this dust and these spider webs on him. He looked like a Halloween ghoul. He looked around; sidestepped the mimbos; looked at me and said, "Do you want me to do this or not"; didn't wait for an answer; walked past Gramps without flinching; walked to Aggie; grabbed her by the shoulders; leaned her back with a hand behind her head, her hair gently meeting the run off from the roof, and planted a big kiss on her lips—dust, spider webs, gentle run-off and all.

I was so happy. It was perfect. Big Bro Nitwit kissed Aggie. She would never live this one down. It was perfect. The scream that followed . . . was mine.

It turned total tick, so totally, totally tick. It was like it never happened. Worse, it happened and Brent wasn't shooting video. There was no picture. I couldn't show it to Beep and Eddie. I couldn't parade it out when she was being a sisters . . . uhhhhh! I thought, okay, at least Brent, Rabbit Poo, Gramps and I saw it, but Brent and Rabbit Poo were trying to help the mimbos up, and Gramps was just laughing. Who knows what he sees and who would believe him? Only Aggie and Big Bro Nitwit and I knew what happened. Well at least there was that? But no, there wasn't that.

Big Bro Nitwit let go of Aggie. It seemed like an awfully long time to hold her. She wasn't saying a thing. She just brushed her wet hair back, a little smile on her face.

Big Bro Nitwit turned to me. "Where's my money?"

"Oh, yeah," I said, fumbling in my pocket for the one dollar. It was the only way to get him there. I thought it was smart that I offered him a really low price because he took it right away.

"It's right here." I pulled out a one.

Aggie looked confused. The hard rain on the roof and the moans on the floor didn't help.

I quickly gave Big Bro Nitwit the money and grabbed his arm to lead him out of the shed.

"Wait! What! . . . Wait!" Aggie wasn't happy. "You paid someone to kiss me?" If she were a train, she would have been ten *steam* locomotives.

"Aaaaa, yeah."

"Mom and Dad are going to kill you!"

"So . . . you kissed Big Bro Nitwit." I thought I could live with that tradeoff. The only thing I couldn't say was that I had evidence of it. Total tick that no one else in the shed even saw it!

"So?" was all she said.

"So, he's Big Bro Nitwit," I said.

"So?"

"So!" I was getting a little alarmed. "Big Bro Nitwit feeds his pet fish to the cat; he flips burgers by flipping the whole barbecue; he took a robot full of poopy doll heads to a dance; he threw river rocks onto his sisters head; she was happy to pick her nose; his little brother played base-ball with a bass; his grandmother walked to the post office naked! He's a Nitwit!" There was more, but I was panicked and exhausted.

"Mom and Dad are going to kill you." She was so calm. I was scared. Big Bro Nitwit just stood there. Gramps was laughing, but picking up his sponges, and Brent and Rab-bit Poo were helping Andrew and Robbie wake up. They wanted nothing to do with Eddie. I think they were simply going to roll him into the storm. Everything was a mess, a mess I was going to have to clean up: the sponges, the trash-can, the dead cat parts, the kiss that was and wasn't, but still at least it happened.

I bet you have no idea what happened or what was said next. Go ahead; give it a guess. I bet you have no idea. Here it is. My perfect plan shattered like a crystal carnival prize dropped on soda and spit stained macadam.

"You kissed Big Bro Nitwit," I said again.

"Yeah," said Aggie. She was getting assertive.

"You kissed Big Bro Nitwit," I said a little weaker.

"Yeah." She stuck out her chin and gave one of those challenging headshakes. "Well . . . he's a good kisser." She tapped me on the chin with her knuckles.

Whaaaat? Whaaaaaaaat? She liked it. She *liked* it! I can't believe it. She liked kissing Big Bro Nitwit.

Aggie grabbed Big Bro Nitwit and yanked the single out of his hand. "A dollar? A dollar! You paid Big Bro Nitwit a dollar to kiss me!" She turned to Big Bro Nitwit before I could say anything.

"I'm only worth a dollar?"

Big Bro Nitwit, in control of every word, said, "I would have kissed you for nothing."

WHAAAAAAAAAAAAAAAAAAAAAAAAAAAAT!

Aggie blushed. I've never seen my sister blush. She sort of put her hand up to his chest.

WHAAAAAAAAAAAAAAAAAAAAAAAAAAAAAT!

She gave him a look. Big Bro Nitwit looked taller. I was two inches high. Big Bro Nitwit walked out into the heavy rain and disappeared. That was it.

Aggie turned around, gave me a smile, and left.

Uhhhhh, Sisters! Uhhhhh. Uhhhhh. Uhhhhh. Uhhhhh. Uhhhhh!!!

"Beep . . . Beep . . . Beep! What the beep happened here?" Beep and Eddie shuffled in, soaking wet. I said nothing.

The mimbos finally rose, cleaned themselves off, and looked around like things would be explained. Gramps let one go and laughed. Brent and The Hero Rabbit Poo took the mimbos over to the house. Why wasn't he shooting video? I so want to give him a monkey-scrub. Gramps secured his sponges, let another one go, laughed, and left. I looked at my friends and said nothing. What could I say.

It is awful. Gramps has a belly full of burrito. We are in the tents tonight. It's raining. I have to clean up the mess here in the shed. I have to cover the toy train. I have to collect all the doll heads. I have to get Beep a new dead cat. I don't have a video. I don't have any reliable witnesses. I have a sister . . . uhhhhh, who said that Big Bro Nitwit was a good kisser. Could you have guessed that? I bet none of you would have guessed that. This is so tick! It is all so tick—sisters, for sure, uhhhhh! And Nitwits . . . oh Nitwits, especially one Nitwit. I so have to get Big Bro Nitwit!

Everything, everything is so totally tick!

So if you are ever asked: "Did Joe's sister kiss a Nitwit?"

She did . . . and she liked it . . . and it's so so so totally totally totally tick.

Nitwits!!!

I think that goat is somewhere here in the shed. I'm just going to take off my pants and hang them up . . .

Acknowledgments

This is how it happened: I had finished writing <u>The Nitwits Come to Town</u> and I read to my son, Joe, the final five chapters. When I finished, he went ballistic. "You can't do that!" he said. At first I was a little miffed and disappointed but then my bride told me that the only reason he was acting that way was because he was invested in the characters. Is there a better compliment? Well yeah! Earlier in the writing, my son was on the computer reading the manuscript, which he was not supposed to be doing, and when I asked him what he was doing, he simply waved me away and kept reading. Now that is the greatest compliment a dad could get!

Thank you Joe for enjoying what your dad has written. Thank you Christine for encouragement, understanding, faith, and perspective. None of this is finished without your love. Thank you Nicholas for playing on the iPad, sleeping, watching Sprout, and at this writing, pushing the ottoman toward the TV, climbing it, and pulling down two speakers, an Xbox remote, two books and an AM antenna. Allowing me to focus has been a great help .

Thank you Matt Duclos for the cover photo; thank you Aubrey Duclos for letting your then fiancé free twice to do the shoots. Thank you Grandma Theresa and Grandma Florence for watching the boys. Thank you Dean Lorey for telling me in a casual conversation when I spoke of a writing idea: "Well, then write it." Simple but true. Thank you Elizabeth Lorey for reading a manuscript and appreciating the simple straightforward language. Thank you Warren Leonard, who, in another casual talk about the book, helped me better frame the story by simply stating: "So, it's a revenge arc."

I think that many of us over think writing, but from a simple wave of a hand, to a simple remark, to simply helping a writer write makes this acknowledgment page a simple joy.

Thank you everyone who kept asking me when a new book would be out . . . here it is.

Gramps walked into the shed to check on his motion activated cameras. . . .

18355862R00086

Made in the USA
Charleston, SC
29 March 2013